THE KILLING IN THE CAFÉ

A Fethering Mystery

Simon Brett

CRÈME de la CRIME

This first world edition published 2015
in Great Britain and 2016 in the USA by
Crème de la Crime, an imprint of
SEVERN HOUSE PUBLISHERS LTD of
19 Cedar Road, Sutton, Surrey, England, SM2 5DA.
Trade paperback edition first published 2016
in Great Britain and the USA by
SEVERN HOUSE PUBLISHERS LTD.

British Library Cataloguing in Publication Data

Brett, Simon author.
  The killing in the cafe. – (A Fethering mystery)
  1. Seddon, Carole (Fictitious character)–Fiction. 2. Jude
  (Fictitious character : Brett)–Fiction. 3. Fethering
  (England : Imaginary place)–Fiction. 4. Women private
  investigators–England–Fiction. 5. Detective and mystery
  stories.
  I. Title II. Series
  823.9'2-dc23

ISBN-13: 978-1-78029-081-2 (cased)
ISBN-13: 978-1-78029-565-7(trade paper)
ISBN-13: 978-1-78010-729-5 (e-book)

All Severn House titles are printed on acid-free paper.

Severn House Publishers support the Forest Stewardship Council™ [FSC™],
the leading international forest certification organisation.
All our titles that are printed on FSC certified paper carry the FSC logo.

MIX
Paper from
responsible sources
FSC® C013056
www.fsc.org

Typeset by Palimpsest Book Production Ltd.,
Falkirk, Stirlingshire, Scotland.
Printed and bound in Great Britain by
TJ International, Padstow, Cornwall.

To Michael,
with many thanks for being such
a great agent and friend
for over forty years

ONE

'That's a word that's the real kiss of death.' Carole Seddon pronounced it with distaste. '"Community".'

'Don't be so cynical,' said Jude.

'I'm not being cynical. I'm being realistic. I've never encountered anything beginning with the word "community" that wasn't a complete disaster. "Community Action" . . . "Community Arts" . . . "Community Politics" . . . "Community Health" . . . They're all shorthand for something that doesn't work.'

'Oh, come on.' Jude was used to her neighbour sounding off, but she really felt she had to challenge this sweeping generalization. 'I've got a lot of friends in the NHS who put in ridiculous hours on Community Health projects and are extremely—'

'All right, all right.' It wasn't in Carole's nature to concede that she was wrong, but she did redefine her criticisms. 'I was talking about "community" at the local level. Where projects are taken on by amateurs rather than professionals, and the amateurs almost invariably mess things up.'

'Well, I'm not sure that—'

'You don't have to look any further than right here in Fethering. Can you name any village project that had the word "community" in front of it and wasn't a total failure?'

'Um, I'm sure there have been—'

'There, you see, you can't,' said Carole with a grin of triumph. 'It's like the word "Big". That used to be a perfectly simple adjective meaning that something was large in size. Now the word's shoved in front of every half-baked project that anyone dreams up and it's supposed to . . . I don't know what . . . to make something intrinsically boring sound trendy and "of the moment". Huh. Do you remember that daft idea that was called "The Big Society", a hopeless scheme to replace the professional services the government had cut by the efforts of unpaid volunteers who hadn't a clue about . . .'

And Carole was off again on another of her rants. Jude smiled inwardly and thought, not for the first time, how unlikely their friendship was. Though about the same age, at that stage of life when women are (inaccurately) said to become invisible, they couldn't have looked more different. Carole Seddon was tall and whippet-thin, with a forbidding helmet of grey hair and pale blue eyes that looked out quizzically – and frequently disapprovingly – from behind rimless glasses. She dressed in clothes which she hoped did not draw attention to her.

Jude, by contrast, was just on the right side between voluptuous and blousy. Her hair was blonde or blonded (no one had ever thought to ask), always piled up on her head and insecurely secured by bands, clips, slides or whatever else she happened to find on her dressing table when she got up. Her eyes were brown and she went through life with an easy sensuality which, in spite of her bulk, men still found irresistible. She dressed in floaty layers of garments and a profusion of scarves.

After a very varied life, which had included two marriages (both childless and both now defunct), stints as a model, an actress and a restaurateur, Jude now operated as a healer. Though she found the work draining and at times frustrating, she was convinced she had found her vocation.

Carole had retired, rather earlier than she would have wished, from the Civil Service, and moved to live full-time in Fethering. She had had quite a high-powered job at the Home Office. Divorced from a very annoying nitpicker of a man called David, she had an adult only son called Stephen, a daughter-in-law Gaby and a much-adored granddaughter called Lily. Gaby was again pregnant, due to give birth in a few weeks at the end of October. So the prospect of becoming a grandmother for the second time was tending to preoccupy Carole. In fact, in some ways it was a relief for Jude to hear her neighbour going on about something other than the forthcoming baby. Like the shortcomings of initiatives prefaced by the word 'community'.

That Sunday evening the two women were sitting in an alcove in Fethering's only pub, the Crown and Anchor. Each had a large glass of New Zealand Sauvignon Blanc. (They had used always to drink Chilean Chardonnay, but had quite suddenly gone off that buttery taste in favour of a crisper white. For a few weeks this innovation had confused the Crown and Anchor's scruffy and bearded landlord, Ted Crisp. It was rare in Fethering for things as momentous as Carole and Jude's drinking habits to change.)

Jude was getting down her glass quicker than Carole, at least partly because she wasn't talking so much. Through the pub windows from the alcove where they sat, Jude could see the sea, the English Channel, shelving very slowly in this part of West Sussex. The tide was out, exposing acres of cement-coloured sand. In the late afternoon there were a few hardy families still playing on the beach, pretending in a very English way that the weather had not turned autumnal. It wasn't actually raining, but the leaden clouds suggested that situation might only be a stay of execution. The children with the families were all very small. The older ones had gone back to school. And soon the little ones would be taken back to their holiday accommodation for suppers, baths and beds.

It was the fourth of October, Jude's birthday, but in their long acquaintance she had never told her neighbour of the date's significance. This was not because Jude had a secretive nature – rather the reverse – but Carole had never mentioned her own birthday. And Jude knew that knowing the date of her friend's would throw Carole into a state of social consternation. How involved should she be in the celebration of the event? What level of expense would be the appropriate outlay for a present? Such questions, Jude knew, could upset Carole's hard-won equilibrium.

Besides, Jude had never made a big deal of birthdays. During her marriages and her longer affairs, they had been celebrated by *tête-à-tête* dinners with the man of the moment, but she didn't feel the need for such indulgence when she was on her own. Because her sitting room doubled as a consulting room, any cards that arrived were displayed upstairs in her bedroom. And otherwise the day was marked only by phone calls and emails from close friends and former lovers.

Of course being born on the fourth of October meant that, for people to whom such things are important, she was a Libran. Jude herself, to whom such things were not without importance, was content to be a Libran and thought she was a fairly typical representative of the sign. Tactful, romantic, able to see both sides of the story . . . yes, she did seem to have some of the positive Libran qualities. As to the negative ones – lazy, indecisive, self-indulgent – yes, at times she could own up to them as well.

The issue which had got Carole so aerated that Sunday evening concerned one of Fethering's two cafés. The Seaview, a glassed-in structure on the edge of the beach, did a busy trade during the summer supplying tourists with battered fish, dry burgers, chips, chips, more chips and endless pots of tea. Though open all the year round, it was generally shunned by the upmarket locals (though the older generation of 'common people' from the Downside council estate continued to patronize it for fish suppers and endlessly eked-out pots of tea).

A venue more in tune with Fethering's middle-class sensibilities was Polly's Cake Shop. Also open all the year round, a casual visitor might at first believe that the place had been unchanged since the 1950s or even earlier. The few American tourists who came to Fethering thought with ecstasy that they had stumbled on a genuine piece of 'Olde England'. They loved the rough white plaster of the interior, they loved the oak beams, they loved the horse brasses and warming pans that hung from them. They were overwhelmed by the red and white gingham tablecloths and the tiered silver cake stands. And when they were approached by wait-resses in black with a frilly white aprons and frilly white caps offering them a menu of toasted teacakes, cucumber sandwiches, homemade coconut kisses and sponge fancies, they thought they'd died and gone to heaven. They knew for certain that they were part of the authentic English tea-shop experience they had witnessed in so many television adaptations of Agatha Christie. Only the appear-ance of Hercule Poirot himself could have made the experience more complete.

It would have been cruel to disillusion them, to point out that until the 1990s the café on Fethering Parade had been a butcher's shop, that the oak beams and other period impedimenta had been grafted on as part of a shrewd marketing campaign. And that all of the café's 'homemade' fare was delivered every morning from a specialist supplier in Brighton.

The owner of Polly's Cake Shop was a woman, but she wasn't called Polly. The name was just another bit of window dressing, with possible echoes of the old nursery rhyme, 'Polly, Put the Kettle On'. The café was owned by an unsentimental woman called Josie Achter. Jude had met Josie through a mutual friend who conducted a Pilates class that Josie attended. Like most Fethering residents,

Jude had also met the owner when enjoying the delights – in Jude's case particularly the éclairs – of Polly's Cake Shop.

Josie Achter, Jude discovered – though from local gossip rather than the woman herself – had invested all of her divorce settlement into the business and exchanged the five-bedroomed house in Esher that she'd shared with her inadequate husband for the cramped flat above the café. There she had brought up her daughter Rosalie until the girl went to college in Brighton to study Hospitality and Catering. And, at the end of her course, though she no longer lived with her mother, Rosalie worked with her in the business. Then after some years Josie, who must by then have been in her late sixties, announced that she was going to retire.

Fethering was rife with rumours that mother and daughter had had a row, but no one actually knew what had happened between them (though lack of information had never inhibited anyone in the village from having an opinion about anything and everything). The only certain facts that emerged were that Rosalie was not going to take over the business, and Josie was going to sell up.

There not being an enormous amount to talk about in Fethering, once the weather and house prices had been dealt with, this news prompted fierce debate. People who had never patronized Polly's Cake Shop became very concerned about 'saving this valuable amenity for the village.' Rumours proliferated about who the purchaser of the property was likely to be. As was standard procedure in such cases, someone claimed to have heard that the premises were to reopen as a sex shop. A more likely conjecture was that it would become another estate agent's. (While other businesses closed with some regularity, there always seemed to be room for another estate agent.)

Equally groundless suspicions were voiced that Polly's Cake Shop was to become an upmarket restaurant under the control of a well-known television chef. This idea that it might continue as a catering outlet gave rise to the inevitable rumour that the place was to become a McDonald's (a prospect that caused much fluttering in the bourgeois dovecotes of Fethering).

And quick on the heels of that came the positive assertion, from somebody who knew as little about the true situation as anyone else in the village, that Polly's Cake Shop was going to become a branch of Starbucks.

This possibility led to considerable outrage and a letter to the *Fethering Observer*, spelling out the threat of 'a genuinely local business becoming an identikit branch of an international, over-priced conglomerate with an idiosyncratic attitude to paying British taxes.'

Soon a 'Save Polly's Cake Shop' campaign had been started. An Open Meeting of the usual suspects among Fethering's busybodies was held, and it was proposed that an action committee should be formed (again no doubt of the usual suspects). The personnel of that body, together with the appointment of a Chair and other officers would be decided at their next meeting, but it was at that first one that the possibility was raised of the village taking over Polly's Cake Shop as a 'Community Project'.

And that was the news which had prompted Carole Seddon's tirade that October Sunday afternoon in the Crown and Anchor.

TWO

J ude had suggested they stay in the pub to eat, but Carole insisted that she had in the fridge the 'perfectly adequate remains of a chicken salad' she'd made on the Friday. She didn't also say that the real reason she wanted to get home was to watch a Sunday evening television series featuring nuns and midwives to which she had become secretly addicted.

So home they went: Jude to her house, Woodside Cottage (though so far as anyone could tell there had never been a wood anywhere near it), and Carole next door to High Tor (though there wasn't a tor within a hundred and fifty miles of Fethering).

While Carole settled down with her perfectly adequate salad for an evening of prayer and placentas, Jude found the light on the answering machine flashing when she entered her sitting room. The message was from one of her clients, Sara Courtney, who sounded to be in a really bad way.

Sara had come to her a couple of years before, on the edge of a serious nervous breakdown and contemplating suicide. In her early forties, she had just come to the end of a very long cohabiting relationship with the chef of the Brighton restaurant she co-owned. The door to her future, which she had thought would at some point involve marriage and children, had been slammed in her face.

So she had not only taken an emotional knock but, as a partner in the business, had also lost her livelihood. Her former partner had subsidized the restaurant by taking on huge loans which Sara didn't know about, and also to subsidize his cocaine habit, which she didn't know about either. She had thought his 'unwinding in a club after a long evening over a hot stove' had involved alcohol at the worst. How wrong she had been. The result was that the restaurant into which she had invested all of her savings had to be sold to settle the debts her former partner had run up.

Her sense of identity had also been challenged. Sara Courtney had always prided herself on being self-reliant. She had worked her own way up in the catering trade, never relying on the financial support of any man. So the loss of the restaurant also took away her *raison d'être*.

As a result of this double private and professional battering, she had completely lost confidence in every aspect of herself. She was delusional and seemed to have a very tentative hold on her sanity. She lost the certainty that a healthy mind can distinguish the real from the imaginary. Ugly fantasies filled her days, and nightmares kept waking her at night. She had started self-harming; her forearms, which she always kept covered in public, were ragged with scars.

Jude, who'd never suffered under the illusion that her style of healing was a complete cure for everything, had despatched Sara first to her GP, who'd prescribed a course of anti-depressants. As these began to dilute the patient's more self-destructive impulses, Jude had started a series of healing sessions designed to bolster her confidence.

These had continued over some months and were soon showing positive results. From the almost catatonic state of despair in which Sara had first visited Woodside Cottage, she was starting to see the possibility of life continuing, though not perhaps in the way she had envisaged that it might in the past.

She was still very fragile, but she did at least manage to get a job, working as a waitress in Polly's Cake Shop. This was, of course, way below her skills level, but it was a step in the right direction. Josie Achter had been impressed by her new employee's efficiency and understanding of the business and had increased her responsibilities until she was acting virtually as an assistant manager. Sara was entrusted with the contacts list for all the staff and often ended up working out their shift rotas.

Jude reckoned that Sara Courtney's relapse into emotional wreckage must be something to do with Polly's Cake Shop and the prospect of her losing her job.

She was only half right. When she rang back she heard that Sara's upset had been related to Polly's Cake Shop. But she was not traumatized by the threat to her employment.

She was traumatized because she had seen a dead body there.

THREE

Jude rang back straight away. Sara sounded so distraught that she suggested she come round to Woodside Cottage. When the woman arrived she was hollow-eyed and trembling, in almost as bad a state as she'd been when they first met. At her best Sara Courtney was a very attractive woman, slender with straight black hair and olive-black eyes that suggested some possible Mediterranean heritage. But she was looking far from her best that afternoon.

Jude comforted her with cuddles and green tea, but it still took some time for Sara to calm down sufficiently to be coherent. Patiently Jude kept saying, 'Just wait. Wait till you're ready. Then tell me exactly what you saw.'

Finally Sara managed to give an answer that was not interrupted by hysteria. 'It was last night,' she said. 'When I was tidying up at the end of the day.'

'What time would that be?'

'Last orders half past five on a Saturday and the café closes at six. The waitresses clear the tables and stack the dishwashers. The kitchen staff tidy up in there. It doesn't take long. I should think they were all gone by six thirty. I was just going round checking everything before I set the alarms and locked up.'

'So you were alone in the café?'

'Yes.'

'And was Josie up in the flat? Or Rosalie?'

'No. Josie was in Brighton and it was Rosalie's day off. Anyway, she doesn't live in the flat any more, she's got her own place in Brighton. And she tries to avoid working weekends when she can. So it was just me who saw it.' There was a new level of uncertainty in her voice. Jude remembered it from when Sara had been at her worst, when she had distrusted every thought or image that went through her head; when she literally thought she was going mad.

'And where did you see it?'

'In the store room. Right at the back of the café.'

'The back faces on to the beach?'

'Yes. There's a little yard behind, then a service road, then the beginning of the dunes.'

'I know it. So the store room contains all the stuff that doesn't need refrigeration?'

'Yes. Though there are two big freezers in there as well. And there are shelves full of spare crockery and cutlery, kitchen roll, loo paper, spare light bulbs, everything . . .'

'And yesterday evening a dead body?'

'Yes.' The reminder threatened once again to destabilize Sara Courtney, but she swallowed deeply and went on, 'It was a man. I think he'd been shot.'

'Where was the wound?'

'Oh his right temple. A neat hole.'

'Much blood?'

'Only a trickle. I wiped it clean with my handkerchief.'

'What?'

'I just . . . it seemed awful . . . him lying there, with the blood . . . Somehow I felt I had to wipe it away.'

Jude made no comment. She was glad Carole wasn't there. Her neighbour would have gone all prissy and Home Office at that point, berating Sara for interfering with a crime scene . . . if, of course, it was a crime scene, and not just a product of the woman's heated imagination.

'You didn't recognize the man, Sara?'

'I'd never seen him before.'

'What age was he?'

'Late fifties, early sixties perhaps.'

'Wearing?'

'Jeans and a kind of plaid work shirt.'

'And what, was he just lying on the floor?'

'Yes.'

'You didn't see any signs that he'd been moved there? Any trail of blood or . . .?'

'As I said, there was very little blood. Just the bit on his temple that I wiped off.'

'Hm. What about a gun?'

'Gun?'

'Well, if there was a bullet hole in his temple, presumably the bullet come out of a gun. Did you see any sign of a gun?'

There was an almost imperceptible pause before Sara replied, 'No, no sign of it.'

Jude decided not to question this. Not at that moment, anyway. 'So what did you do?'

'Last night?'

'Yes.'

'I didn't do anything. I went home – and I had a terrible night. Every time I closed my eyes I saw the same image – of the man dead.'

'So you haven't told anyone about what you saw?'

'No, you're the first person.'

'You didn't think of calling the police?'

'My life's complicated enough as it is.'

Which was a strange reply to the question, but Jude didn't pick up on it. Instead she said, 'But surely by now someone else will have seen the body, won't they? I mean, Polly's is open today, isn't it?'

'Oh yes. Sunday's one of our busiest days this time of year. Business makes most of its profit over the weekends.'

'So have you been back there today?'

'Yes. I was scheduled to work all day, but I cried off pretty early, claimed I'd got food poisoning.'

'But did you go back to the store room?'

'Yes. I steeled myself to it. I knew I had to.'

There was a silence. 'And?' Jude prompted.

'And the body wasn't there.'

'Oh?'

'No sign that it ever had been there. And that got me more panicked than if I'd found it again. It made me think back to—'

'To when you first came to see me?'

'Yes. I was worried that my mind was going again, that I was seeing things like I did when . . . You know how quickly one thought leads to another?' Jude nodded. 'And I thought if I'm hallucinating, seeing stuff that isn't there, then I'm not on the way to recovery like I thought I was. Last night I very nearly took a razor to my arm again – only just managed to stop myself. I'm right back where I started and there's no hope for me. I'm finished.'

'Of course you're not, Sara. This isn't the first time you've slipped back, you know that. But you've bounced back before, and you'll bounce back from this too.'

Sara shook her head miserably. 'No, this time I think it's for good.'

'That's what depressives always think. That's what's so dispiriting about the disease. When you go down you can never envisage coming up again. But you will, Sara, you will.'

All that prompted was a wry, disbelieving, humourless grin.

'Tell me, though . . . now, now you've had time to consider it, do you really think you did see the body in the store room last night?'

'Well, I think I did.' She looked very confused. 'I hope I did.'

'Why do you say that?'

'If I didn't, then I really am going mad again.' Jude didn't comment. 'I can't stand it. I haven't got the energy to go through all that again. I think this time I really will have to—'

'Don't even think about it,' said Jude with gentle firmness. 'This is only a minor setback. You're bound to have a few of those. But you will come out of it.'

Sara didn't even nod at this reassurance. Tears, ready to flow again, glinted in her eyes.

Jude, who knew about the savage tricks the mind could play, wondered whether Sara had actually seen anything or not. Certainly, if a murder had happened, and if it ever came to court, she would be the most unreliable of witnesses.

'And sadly, I suppose,' said Jude, 'you don't have any proof of what you saw?'

'Only this.' Sara Courtney reached into her jeans pocket and pulled out a white handkerchief. On it was a rust-coloured bloodstain.

FOUR

'I think, if we could call this meeting to order . . .' The speaker, Commodore Quintus Braithwaite, banged his gavel on the table. He was the kind of man who would always have his own personal gavel.

The Commodore was in fact a relative newcomer to Fethering. That is to say that – though he had been the owner of a large house in the Shorelands Estate to the west of the village for many years – he, his wife Phoebe and their three children had spent very little time there. It was only after his retirement from the Royal Navy that he became a full-time resident. He had quickly become a familiar sight around Fethering, favouring tweed jackets or khaki gilets, open-necked shirts with very large checks and corduroy trousers in burgundy or English mustard yellow. He appeared just to have given up one uniform for another.

And for the past two years he had involved himself in every aspect of village life, bringing to local affairs the organizational skills which had raised him through his career in the Forces. The actual quality of those organizational skills was something on which the Fethering jury was still out.

The latest village initiative in which Quintus Braithwaite was involving himself was the 'Save Polly's Cake Shop' campaign, already shortened to 'SPCS'. Indeed it was he who had written the letter to the *Fethering Observer* about the threat from 'an international, overpriced conglomerate with an idiosyncratic attitude to paying British taxes', also known as Starbucks.

And he was very much taking over the second meeting of the campaign's committee. For a start he had decreed that it should take place at his house, which gave him home advantage. The Shorelands Estate was an exclusive gated community with complicated regulations for its residents as to when they could hang out their washing or mow their lawns. Many of the houses, like the Braithwaites', backed on to the sea, and a good few had sailing dinghies lined up at the ends of their gardens. Quintus Braithwaite, who had commanded considerably larger vessels during his professional life, was an avid sailor and very bossy to anyone who crewed for him (usually his wife Phoebe). He kept his main boat on one of the riverside moorings owned by Fethering Yacht Club, but he also owned a small blue-painted tender with an outboard which was kept at the end of his garden.

The house itself – named, incongruously, 'Hiawatha' – was a big six-bedroomed affair, built in what a 1950s architect had reckoned to be Elizabethan style. This meant there was a lot of red brick, a few supernumerary turrets and far too many tall chimneys twisted like barley sugar. Inside, no attempt had been made to continue the Elizabethan motif. The décor in all of the rooms had the immaculate impersonal gloss which can only be supplied by very expensive interior designers.

They were meeting in the sitting room, a huge space filled with an excess of large sofas. Rather than commanding the sea view, its picture windows faced inland towards the 'Green' at the centre of the Shorelands Estate, but since the thick brocade curtains were closed, nobody missed anything.

For the less well-heeled members of the SPCS campaign group, the house displayed a daunting opulence. Phoebe Braithwaite, a twittery woman in a Liberty print dress whose eyes blinked a lot behind thick glasses, had supplied tea, coffee and biscuits in very fine china. Thrown by the splendour of the venue, few of those present were about to question anything their host proposed.

Jude was there simply to support Sara Courtney. Her client seemed to have settled down after her outburst that Sunday at Woodside Cottage. There had been no more mention of the dead body she had possibly seen in the store room. But ten days on, Jude knew that Sara was still very brittle and might need support when the fate of her place of employment was discussed.

Having called the meeting to order, Commodore Quintus Braithwaite didn't mess around. He moved straight on to the power coup which he had clearly planned. 'Now, what we want to do this evening is to get an action committee in place, so that we can move forward in a constructive manner. At the last meeting I asked for nominations for someone to be Chair of the committee but, since we haven't had any, I feel it my duty to step into the breach. So if we could take a vote on—'

'Just a minute, just a minute.' The interruption came from Arnold Bloom, a Fethering resident whom Jude recognized but didn't know well. He was a small man who habitually wore a frayed suit and tie. Unmarried, he lived in the former fisherman's cottage where he had been born. He still slept in the bed where the birth had taken place. His hair, dark but very thin, was combed down from a central parting in a manner which made it look as if it had been painted on to his bony cranium. Arnold had run the village's small hardware store until the opening of a large Homebase nearby had ended its financial viability. Since then he had taken over Fethering's Crazy Golf course (its title now modernized to Adventure Golf). He had the embittered conviction that the world had done him wrong, and had been Chairman of the Fethering Village Committee for as long as anyone could remember.

'I was at the last meeting, Quintus,' he went on, 'as were a lot of other people present this evening who I'm sure could bear me out on this – and I have no recollection of nominations being asked for Chairman of this SPCS committee.'

'It may not have been said in so many words,' the owner of Hiawatha protested, 'but I think it was implicit in our discussions.'

'I don't think that at all,' said Arnold Bloom. 'All that was said was that at the next meeting we would need to appoint a Chairman.'

'I prefer the word "Chair",' said the Commodore.

'Well, I prefer the word "Chairman". At meetings of the Fethering Village Committee I don't like to be referred to as a piece of furniture.'

'I think you're being rather small-minded, Arnold.'

'Do you? Well, I think I know rather more about the workings of Fethering than you do. I was born in the village; I've lived here all my life.'

'Well, I have owned this house for over thirty years.'

'Not quite the same, though, is it, Quintus? You may have owned the house but you've hardly spent more than the odd week in it.'

'That,' the Commodore responded with some hauteur, 'is because I have been abroad, defending the realm on behalf of Her Majesty Queen Elizabeth the Second.'

'I'm sure she was very grateful to you,' said Arnold Bloom drily, 'but it doesn't change the fact that you know very little about how this village works. We do still have some respect for democracy in this neck of the woods, you know.'

'I too have an enormous respect for democracy. That was another thing I was defending, as well as the realm.'

'Well if, Quintus, you have as much respect for democracy as you claim, why are you trying to ride roughshod over the democratic system to get yourself elected as Chairman of this committee?'

'I am not "riding roughshod". I am offering my services on behalf of the community.'

'Very generous of you. But I still think we should have checked to see whether there are any other nominees for the post of Chairman of the SPCS Action Committee.'

'Well, are there?' The Commodore looked balefully around his sitting room, daring anyone else to put themselves forward. Nobody did. 'Right, it would seem that—'

'Just a minute. If you can put yourself forward, then so can I.'

'You?'

'Yes. I, Arnold Bloom. I am putting myself forward as a candidate for the position of Chairman of the SPCS Action Committee.'

'But you can't do that.'

'Why not? You just did.'

'My situation is entirely different from yours.'

'In what way?'

'You are already Chair of the Fethering Village Committee.'

'Chair*man*, actually.'

'Never mind that. If you were also Chair of the SPCS Action Committee, there would be a clear conflict of interest.'

'No, there wouldn't.'

'Yes, there would.'

'No, there wouldn't.'

Jude was beginning to wonder whether this pantomime crosstalk would go on until the two men ended up hitting each other. But Quintus Braithwaite stopped the bickering and, turning to the assembled throng of the usual suspects, he said, 'Very well, we now have two candidates for the post of Chair of the SPCS Action Committee. Myself, Commodore Quintus Braithwaite, and Arnold Bloom, who, as you all know, is already Chair of—'

'Chair*man* of—'

'*Chair* of the Fethering Village Committee. He claims there would be no conflict of interest were he to take on the role of Chair of both bodies, but I need hardly point out that, should the SPCS Action Committee decide to follow a course which was opposed by the Fethering Village Committee . . .' He spread his arms wide and shrugged. 'Need I say more?'

'Well, I think you should say more if—'

But the Commodore steamrollered over Arnold Bloom's objections. 'Very well, so we'll take this straight to the vote. Will those of you who believe that Arnold Bloom is the right person to take over the task of chairing the SPCS Action Committee please raise your right hands?' Only a few went up. 'And those of you who believe that Commodore Quintus Braithwaite would do a better job in the role, please raise your right hands?'

Maybe, thought Jude, he thinks speaking of himself in the third person makes his total disregard for the democratic process more acceptable? It didn't matter, though. Commodore Quintus Braithwaite had won the vote and was duly elected Chair of the SPCS Action Committee.

'Good,' he said. 'I'm glad that's sorted. And I think the next most important thing we should organize is getting some headed notepaper printed. Nothing impresses or shows the seriousness of any business enterprise more than an effective letterhead. Now there's a stationery printer in London whom my wife Phoebe has used for invitations for charity balls and that kind of thing, and I think we can guarantee that they would produce a stylish letterhead for—'

'Just a minute,' interposed Arnold Bloom. 'Aren't we getting a bit ahead of ourselves here? Yes, we may in time need SPCS notepaper, but we shouldn't be thinking about getting it printed until we know what names are going to be on it.'

'I thought we'd just established,' said the Commodore acidly, 'that I am Chair of the SPCS Action Committee. So obviously my name should go on the letterhead.'

'Yes, but what other names should also be there?'

'I don't think, Arnold, we actually need any other names.'

'But what about the names of the Action Committee's other officers?'

'We don't have any other officers.'

'No, but we will. You're not proposing to run the whole thing on your own, are you, Quintus?'

It was clear to Jude, from the expression on the Commodore's face, that that was exactly what he was proposing to do. 'Well, obviously,' he said, 'I'll need secretarial back-up and—'

'But more than that,' Arnold countered, 'you will rely on the full support of your committee.'

'Well, yes,' the newly elected Chair conceded, 'I'm sure their views on certain topics will be invaluable to my work but—'

'I don't think we can proceed any further until we have appointed the full committee.' Arnold Bloom sat back with some satisfaction. And even more satisfaction when a ripple of agreement went around the room. No one in Fethering could outdo him when it came to procedural protocol. He felt he had won a small but significant victory over Quintus Braithwaite.

A lengthy discussion then ensued as to the optimum number of committee members required. Needless to say, the Commodore had views on this subject too. He also laid down some ground rules, trying to cancel out Arnold Bloom's recent triumph. Without mentioning his rival by name, he said he thought it would be invidious for any member of the Fethering Village Committee to be on the SPCS Action Committee, for the previously mentioned 'conflict of interest' reasons.

On this he didn't get his own way, though. Arnold Bloom spoke eloquently of the need for 'transparent liaison' between the two committees and, experienced in the ways of managing meetings, pushed for a quick vote on the issue. This time, probably because some of those present were feeling guilty for having excluded such a stalwart of Fethering society from the Chairmanship, he won and was duly elected a member of the SPCS Action Committee.

Looking at the faces of the two men, Jude envisaged many conflicts in meetings to come and felt glad that there was no danger of her being involved in their process of oneupmanship.

A long wrangle then ensued as to how many people should be members of the ideal action committee. The Commodore recommended nine, so that in the event of a four-all split, the Chair's casting vote could decide the issue. Arnold Bloom, for reasons which seemed to be nothing more than bloody-mindedness, favoured a larger committee. Thirteen seemed to him to be the ideal number.

This suggestion was vetoed, however, by a woman with the long blonde hair of a flower child from the Sixties. The face framed by this hair suggested that it could well have been in the Sixties when she first started dyeing it.

She identified herself as Flora Claire and objected that thirteen was a 'bad luck number' and it would be, like, really tempting fate to set up the committee on such an inauspicious basis. 'I think we should go with a committee of fifteen,' she said. 'Fifteen is a number which has really good vibes. It's made up of one and five and they are both really sympathetic numbers.'

'But fifteen,' protested Arnold Bloom, 'is too many. In my very extensive experience of committees, with fifteen everything becomes very unwieldy. Thirteen is the perfect number for maximum efficiency.'

'Fifteen, though,' Flora continued, 'is a really auspicious number. Not only is it, like I said, made up of one and five, it's also five times three, and three is like one of the most potent numbers there is. I think we have to go with fifteen.'

Normally the Commodore would have pooh-poohed such a flaky suggestion, but in this case it was an argument against Arnold Bloom so, come the vote, he supported Flora Claire. As did the majority of those present and in that way Braithwaite achieved his first small victory over his rival. And also, to Jude's mind, ended up with a committee which was far too large to be efficient.

Encouraged by his success, though, Quintus next laid down another ground rule. This again was on the grounds of conflict of interest. He decreed that no one who had any involvement in the current ownership or management of Polly's Cake Shop should be allowed on to the committee.

This did not seem to Jude to be too controversial. Neither Josie Achter nor her daughter Rosalie had shown any interest in attending either the first or second meeting of the SPCS. But to her surprise she felt Sara nudge her and heard a whisper in her ear saying, 'Will you stand on the committee for me then?'

'What?' Jude whispered back.

'I'm very concerned about the future of Polly's. I want to be involved in whatever happens to the place. And if I can't be on the committee, then I want someone there rooting for me.'

'Well, I'm not sure that I—'

But she was interrupted by the Commodore asking for nominations for the other vacant positions on the SPCS Action Committee.

This was another characteristic rule-bending ploy. If he'd asked for volunteers, he would have ended up with all of the usual suspects who were on every other committee in Fethering. Asking for nominations might wrong-foot some of them and make for a less predictable line-up.

And the first name to be put forward could certainly not have been predicted. Before she had time to stop her, Jude found herself being nominated by Sara Courtney. Painfully aware of the woman's fragility, she didn't want to raise objections in such a public forum and so, to her hidden fury, found herself duly elected to the SPCS Action Committee.

FIVE

Other nominations were made and the remaining thirteen places on the SPCS Action Committee were quickly filled. Flora Claire had a surprising amount of support in the room and was duly elected.

So was a thin, dry, almost skeletal man – round the seventy mark – who identified himself as Alec Walters, a retired accountant. Because of his professional qualification, and because so few people in the village could even understand a balance sheet, he found himself in the role of Treasurer on virtually every committee in Fethering. And he duly became Treasurer of the SPCS Action Committee.

The role of Secretary was given to Wendy Roote, a stalwart of SADOS, an amateur dramatic group in a nearby village (known more fully as 'Smalting Amateur Dramatic and Operatic Society', and known by local cynics as the 'Saddoes'). She assured the assembled throng that she'd do everything possible for the cause of SPCS 'so long as I'm not in rehearsal.'

Wendy who, like Alec Walters, had clearly served her time on several local committees, asked who would be organizing the Agenda for the next meeting. Quintus Braithwaite, caught on the hop because he hadn't anticipated this question, quickly improvised that any members who wished to put forward items should let the Secretary know about them, and Wendy would ensure that they appeared on the relevant Agenda.

Then a woman who nobody had seen before introduced herself rather breathlessly as Lesley Tarquin. She was dressed in white jeans as tight as tights, and a sort of silver lattice-work top. Her very short hair had actually been dyed white (an unusual thing in Fethering where there was a sufficiency of white hair on display without resorting to chemical enhancement). 'I've only just moved down here from Pimlico. Used to work in PR, so I know all about the "marketing and publicity game". I'm very interested in how much can be achieved coverage-wise through the social-media platforms like Facebook and Twitter.' She spoke with such enthusiasm and apparent expertise that someone very quickly proposed her as a committee member and she was duly appointed to the title of Press Officer.

Having got most of his objectives achieved, with Arnold Bloom's presence on the committee the only minor setback, Commodore Quintus Braithwaite was in expansive mood. He suggested the date of the next meeting to be a fortnight hence – 'got to move along with these things, mustn't let the grass grow under our feet. And it'll be as easy to have it here again, that is' – he deferred to his wife – 'if the management has no objections.'

Phoebe Braithwaite, not for the first time in their married life, assured her husband that she had no objections to what he intended to do anyway.

Arnold Bloom, however, had a predictable argument to put forward. 'Surely it'd be better if our meetings were held on neutral ground? The Fethering Village Committee always meets in the All Saints Church Hall, and that's a more central venue for—'

'I'm not so sure.' Quintus Braithwaite was not going to concede home advantage so easily. 'I've sat on hard seats in too many draughty church halls over the years to want to repeat the experience more than I have to.'

But Arnold had what he thought to be another clinching argument up his sleeve. 'All Saints Church Hall is also a short walk from the Crown and Anchor, where we frequently adjourn for a noggin after meetings of the Fethering Village Committee.'

He had, however, simply played into his opponent's hands. 'Well, that's not a problem,' said Quintus bonhomously. 'Phoebe, you can start pouring the wine straight away.'

His wife dutifully scuttled off into the kitchen.

'Now obviously,' the Chair went on, 'at our next meeting we'll have a proper Agenda and formal discussions, but I think we've achieved a lot tonight, getting our officers and committee in place, and maybe it's the time to draw this evening's proceedings to a close—'

He was fingering his gavel, but was preventing from bashing it on the table by an interruption from Flora Claire. 'I think we should just have a short discussion about what, if we take over Polly's as a Community Café, we want it to be.'

'Well, we want it to be a Community Café,' said the Commodore a little testily.

'Yes, but what kind of events do we want to take place there?' Flora persisted.

'We don't want events, we want people drinking tea and coffee and eating sticky cakes.'

'Oh, but there's so much more we could do with the place.'

'Like what?'

'Well, it could become a venue for people to relax in . . .'

'Yes, fine. They can relax while they have their tea and coffee and sticky cakes.'

'No, but I meant it could become a more *spiritual* place.'

'What?' asked Quintus Braithwaite with considerable foreboding.

'Like a Mindfulness Centre.'

'A Mindfulness Centre?' The sceptical tone of his echo was one that Jude had heard often in reaction to her claims to be a healer.

But Flora Claire seemed unaware of it. 'Yes, everyone's into Mindfulness these days, and it'd be great to have a resource right here in Fethering for—'

The Commodore had heard enough. 'I think the basic aim of the SPCS should be to save the café in its existing state – as a café. If there were, later down the line, a majority on the committee who then wanted it to be used as a venue for other activities – and I rather doubt if there would be – then that would clearly be something to discuss at a subsequent committee meeting.'

This had the desired effect of shutting Flora up. But not, Jude felt sure, for ever. Another ongoing conflict to develop during future meetings. Not only the Chair against Arnold Bloom but also the Chair against Flora Claire. Jude wondered gloomily why she hadn't been quick-footed enough to avoid being elected on to the SPCS Action Committee. And how quickly she could decently get off it. She loathed committees.

Phoebe Braithwaite was already appearing from the kitchen with a tray of wine glasses filled with white and red, and Quintus's gavel was once again poised to descend when another interruption came, this time from Arnold Bloom.

'I feel, Mr Chairman,' he said, deliberately avoiding any shortening of the title, 'that there is one thing we on the committee should focus on as soon as possible, and that is finance.'

'No worries there,' said the Commodore dismissively. 'We've just appointed a Treasurer.'

'Yes, it was not that level of finance that I was talking about. I have no doubt that Alec will be an excellent Treasurer for the SPCS Action Committee, as he has been an excellent Treasurer for so many other local societies, but the finance I was referring to was on a rather bigger scale.'

'Oh, really?' Quintus Braithwaite's tone was edging towards rude. He wanted to get the committee meeting finished as soon as possible so that he could impress those present with the lavishness of Hiawatha's hospitality.

'Running Polly's Cake Shop as a Community Enterprise is an admirable idea,' Arnold Bloom continued, 'but the fact remains that the community does not own the premises. And I think before we go any further in planning how the venue would be run, we should confront this rather large elephant in the room. How are we going to raise the money required to buy their property?'

'We could rent it,' came the reply from the Chair, who had only just thought of that.

'We could rent it only if the person who owns the freehold is agreeable to having us rent it.'

'And who would that person be?' asked Quintus Braithwaite casually, unwilling to reveal the inadequacy of his researches into the project.

'Well, currently Josie Achter owns it. But I've heard rumours that she's very keen to sell up and might not be open to the idea of renting the place out.'

'Then we should definitely find out if that is her position or not.'

Arnold Bloom nodded. 'That is exactly what I was about to suggest. I feel investigation of that matter should be initiated, before the next meeting indeed, so that the outcome can be reported on at that meeting . . . I think it's vital that we should find out the views of the current owner of Polly's Cake Shop on its future.'

'We're not going to be bound by what she thinks,' the Commodore protested.

'That will rather depend on whether we are in any position to dictate terms – in other words, returning to the elephant in the room, whether we can somehow raise the funding to purchase the freehold.'

'Don't you think it possible,' interposed Flora Claire, 'that Josie might be prepared to rent the place to us?'

'We could certainly ask her about that,' said Arnold. But he didn't sound optimistic.

'Or maybe,' Flora went on, 'she might be prepared to lower the price a bit . . . "for the sake of Fethering"?'

Jude's reaction to that suggestion would have been, 'Dream on', and others present were equally dismissive of the idea.

Arnold Bloom said diplomatically that every avenue should be investigated. 'And I'm sure that sounding out the current owner would be a tactful exercise. We might find that Josie Achter is a strong supporter of the Community Project we are envisaging.'

From what Jude had heard of the woman, this sounded unlikely. Nor did it seem any likelier that the community of Fethering would be able to raise the kind of money needed to buy the café. In fact, she felt sure that the SPCS Action Committee was one of those local initiatives which would pretty soon die of attrition. The enthusiasm with which it had been set up would melt away in the face of reality. And she for one wouldn't feel much regret when that happened. She'd only come to Hiawatha to support Sara. She'd much rather be spending her Wednesday evening in the Crown and Anchor.

Alec Walters, the recently elected Treasurer, now thought it was time to put his oar in. 'If Josie Achter had any interest in the future of her property, one would have thought that she'd have appeared at one of our SPCS meetings. But she has appeared at neither.'

'That's a good point,' said Quintus Braithwaite, anticipating the rejection of Arnold Bloom's suggestion.

'But I still think,' his opponent went on, 'that ascertaining her views on the situation would be a necessary preliminary step. It's important we know whether we're likely to receive co-operation or obstruction from her.'

'Very well,' the Chair of the committee said shortly. 'We'll put it to the vote. Will those in favour of checking out Josie Achter's attitude to what we're doing please raise your right hands?'

To his annoyance he saw that more of those present supported Arnold Bloom than him. It was then discussed which committee member should make the approach to Josie Achter to find out her position. Sara Courtney announced that Jude knew the woman in question through a Pilates connection.

And to Jude's annoyance she found out that not only was she on the SPCS Action Committee, she had also been delegated by it to approach Josie Achter.

SIX

The next morning, the Thursday, Carole Seddon had a call from a very worried-sounding Stephen. Her son told her that his wife Gaby had suffered a small amount of bleeding and was in hospital. The doctors had reassured him that this was not unusual at her stage of pregnancy, and if it was a sign of labour starting, the baby was sufficiently developed to be viable. But he didn't sound reassured.

Carole immediately asked if there was anything she could do, like looking after her granddaughter Lily while Stephen was at the hospital, and it turned out that that was exactly the offer he had hoped she would make.

She threw a few overnight things into a bag, taking four days' worth of underwear because she didn't know how long her stay in Fulham would be. And then she was faced with the problem of what to do with her Labrador Gulliver. As she went downstairs to her immaculate kitchen, he looked up from his favourite position in front of the Aga reproachfully, as if to say, 'You nearly forgot about me, didn't you?'

There were kennels she had used before, most recently when she went with Jude for a fortnight's holiday in Turkey, but they weren't close by and she didn't know whether they'd take on dogs for an undefined period. So instead Carole hurried round from High Tor to Woodside Cottage to ask if Jude could look after Gulliver.

This was not completely unprecedented. Her neighbour had stepped into the breach before and, when she heard the situation, immediately volunteered to take the dog.

Carole said he could be left in High Tor if Jude had to go out or had a client to treat and that it might be simpler to feed him in her house because all his stuff was there. 'And he needs a good walk twice a day. As you know, I tend to take him on Fethering Beach before seven every morning . . .' She caught the expression in Jude's eye. '. . . though it is of course up to you what time you take him out . . . and indeed where you take him.'

'I'll take care of him, don't worry.'

Gulliver seemed to understand her tone of voice – or maybe he'd just recognized the word 'walk' that his owner had uttered. He looked up lovingly at Jude and wagged his sand-coloured tail.

Carole made a considerable drama of giving Jude a key to High Tor. It might have been imagined that, being so close, the two neighbours would have a copy of each other's keys on a permanent basis, but that didn't take into account Carole Seddon's attitude to security. Though she always had a key to Woodside Cottage on a hook in her kitchen, she only lent one of hers to Jude on an emergency-by-emergency basis. If she were honest with herself, this was because she thought her neighbour laid-back to the point of being scatter-brained, and worried that the key might get lost under the piles of cushions and throws in her cluttered sitting room. Or, worse, might be stolen by one of Jude's flakier clients.

Anyway, the arrangements were quickly made. Jude was surprised at how panicked her neighbour seemed to be by the news about Gaby, but she didn't get a chance to ask further questions. A very tight-faced Carole was soon driving in her showroom-clean Renault towards Fulham.

With the result that Jude hadn't had time to tell her about the previous night's meeting of the SPCS Action Committee at Hiawatha.

There had been no call from Carole by the time Jude left Woodside Cottage on the Friday morning, so she just hoped that no news was good news. Her destination was Polly's Cake Shop. With Sara Courtney as her go-between, and playing on their connection through the Pilates class, Jude had fixed a meeting with Josie Achter. She was still annoyed at having been dragooned on to the committee, but she was determined to discharge efficiently the duties that she had been given, and then work out her exit strategy.

The message that came back from Sara had suggested Josie Achter was not about to be very accommodating. Friday was a busy day for her. The only time she could make a meeting was at eight in the morning. As the supplicant, Jude was in no position to argue.

They had agreed that Sara would let her in at seven forty-five for her meeting with Josie at eight o'clock, which was also the time at which Polly's Cake Shop opened to the general public.

Once inside, Jude said, 'Well, can you show me?'

'Show you what?' asked Sara, already changed ready for work into her black dress, white apron and cap.

'The store room. Where you saw the dead body.'

The young woman blushed. 'Oh, I don't know about that.'

'You don't know whether you can let me see it?'

'No. I don't know whether I saw it.'

'The body?'

She nodded awkwardly. 'Yes, I . . . I was in a bad state then. You know, like when I first came to consult you. I was seeing things.'

'You gave me a pretty convincing description of the man you found.' Sara looked even more uneasy. 'And then there was the blood on your handkerchief . . .'

'Yes.'

'Have you put that in the wash?'

A shake of the head. 'It still worries me . . . the thought of going back to where I was when . . . you know, mentally.'

'Yes. You're not going back there, Sara,' said Jude forcefully.

'But if I'm starting to see things that aren't there again . . .'

'And you seriously think it wasn't there? You didn't see a body at all?'

'No, I'm sure I didn't.'

But Sara still sounded confused and Jude wasn't so sure. 'Well, whether you did or didn't, you can still show me the store room.'

Silently, buttoning up objections, Sara Courtney did as she was told. She led Jude through the kitchen, where a whistling chef was opening plastic boxes of bacon and sausages ready for the breakfast orders. He waved cheerily at the two of them. 'Morning, gorgeous,' he said to Sara.

'Morning, Hammo. This is my friend Jude.'

'Morning, other gorgeous,' he said. 'I'm Hammo.' He wore a striped bandana tight round gingerish hair and his green eyes flickered with mischief.

'Pleased to meet you.'

He must have read a slight hesitation in her voice and felt an explanation was needed. 'Yes, Hammo. Unusual name, I admit. And it's nothing to do with the quality of my ham sandwiches. It comes from school – take too long to explain but its origin follows impeccable twelve-year-old logic.'

'I'll take your word for that.'

'Can I get you a coffee or something, Jude?'

'No, just had some, thank you.' And no doubt, she reckoned, she'd be offered more when she got up to Josie's flat.

Hammo looked up at the sound of someone else coming in through the street door. 'Ooh, I'm spoilt for choice this morning, aren't I? Another gorgeous woman coming into my kitchen. And a highly intelligent one too.'

'You don't fool me, Hammo,' said an approaching female voice, smoked to a turn by cigarettes. 'I know you only want me for my body.'

Jude turned to face the newcomer. A tall woman with grey hair bundled into an old-fashioned ballet dancer's bun, she wore a bright orange coat and pink shiny boots.

'Morning, Binnie,' said Sara and Hammo together. 'This is Binnie Swales who—'

But the woman called Binnie interrupted the introduction. 'I know you. Jude, isn't it? You like éclairs.'

'I certainly do. Yes, you've often served me over the years.'

'Over the years?' Binnie blew out a sceptically thin column of air. 'Yes, a good few years they've been too. I've been here since before the Flood.'

'Oh, you mean three or four years ago, when those freak high tides—'

'I was referring to the biblical one,' said Binnie. Then she set off towards the Ladies. 'I must just slip into something less garish,' she said.

Hammo and Sara grinned at each other. Binnie Swales was clearly something of a character around Polly's Cake Shop.

Hammo returned to his breakfast preparations as Sara said, 'Come on. Have a look.' And opened the store-room door.

It was exactly as she had described it. Two large upright freezers against one wall and deep wooden shelves on the other. A lot of mostly janitorial supplies stacked up on them. The only food items were big boxes of dried packaged items like crisps, noodles and pasta. The whole area was scrubbed spotless. Any residual thoughts in Jude's mind that there might be visible evidence of a corpse having rested on the store-room floor nearly a fortnight before were quickly dispelled.

She looked around the space. 'And where did you say you saw the gun?'

It was a cheap shot which she wasn't very proud of, taking Sara off balance like that, but it worked, eliciting the reply, 'On the windowsill by the back door.'

'Right.' Jude moved quickly on before Sara became aware of her lapse. 'I noticed the door wasn't locked. Does everyone have access to this room?'

'Yes, of course. Whoever needs to stock up from something in here, they just come and get it.'

Jude nodded. Apart from the one through which they had entered, there was another more solid-looking door at the far end. 'That's the one that leads out to the beach?' she asked.

'Yes. Well, it leads out to the yard, then the service road, then the dunes.'

'Can you open it?'

'Sure.' Sara pushed a horizontal bar on the door and it swung open. The wind was riding up over Fethering Beach and the smell of the sea was almost overpowering.

'Can the door be opened from the outside?'

'Not without a key, no.'

'And is it on the burglar alarm system?'

'Yes. When that's set, it works for all the entrances to the café.'

'And what about the flat upstairs? Is that on the same system?'

'I don't know. I've never thought to ask. But I would assume so.'

Jude wandered out into the little yard. It was tidy and uncluttered. Wide gates leading to the service road were held closed by a chain and padlock. When opened they would have allowed delivery lorries to back in to get as near as possible to the store room. They could also presumably, if required, have allowed a corpse to enter and depart.

She turned back and looked into the dark eyes of Sara Courtney. 'Did you really see a dead body in there?' she asked.

Sara broke eye contact. 'I prefer not to think about it.'

Which was, Jude reflected, a rather strange answer. Particularly from someone who had just inadvertently admitted to having seen a gun on the store room's windowsill.

The sitting room of Josie Achter's flat looked out over the grey expanse of Fethering Beach, but its interior was functional rather than comfortable. Though everything was perfectly clean and tidy, the place looked somehow unloved. There were no family photographs on display and the pictures on the walls appeared to have no personal resonance. The lack of emotional investment in the place was emphasized by the cardboard boxes on the floor into which Josie had been packing books.

Jude's expectation of being offered coffee was not realized and the vibes she was getting from the owner of Polly's Cake Shop suggested that her presence there was something of an imposition.

After truncated pleasantries about Pilates, Jude cut straight to the chase. 'You are aware, I hope, Josie, of a plan to run Polly's as a Community Project?'

'I've heard rumours about it. Not much happens in Fethering you don't hear rumours about.'

Her voice had a nasal twang. She was short. Her purple trousers and tight black woollen top seemed to restrain her body, almost corset it. A gold motif round the neck of the top was echoed by the gold leather of her sandals. Her hair was cut short, black with a purplish sheen.

'And what do you think about it?'

Josie shrugged. 'What does it matter what I think about it?'

'Well, you are the current owner of the place.'

'Yes, but as soon as I get the price I want for it, I'll be out of here.'

'And you don't care about its future?'

'Why should I?'

'Well, you've invested so much time and effort into it.'

'It's my business. What is a business except for something you invest time and effort into? Then when you decide to leave, you want to cash in.'

'Are you telling me you don't care whether it continues to operate as a café or not?'

'There's a logic for it to continue operating as a café. Maybe I can get a better price if I sell it as a going concern. If someone offers me more, I don't care what they want to do with the place.'

Jude dared to joke, 'There's a local rumour it's going to be sold and reopen as a sex shop. Would you approve of that?'

Her question only prompted another shrug. 'Be no skin off my nose.'

'But don't you feel any responsibility for your regular customers?'

'Why should I? Do they feel any responsibility for me?'

'Not responsibility perhaps, but they feel a loyalty to you.'

'Do they? Do you think they would notice if suddenly one day they don't see me in the café, they see another owner? It wouldn't make a single one of them blow the froth off their cappuccino.'

'You don't make it sound as if you've enjoyed your time running Polly's Cake Shop?'

'It's a business. It's my work. Why should I enjoy my work? The vast majority of people in this country don't enjoy theirs.'

'No, but surely in the hospitality business you have to maintain at least a front of being welcoming?'

'And that's exactly what I have maintained – a front. Listen, Jude, I bought this business at the end of a very sticky divorce, when my bastard ex-husband and his bastard lawyer screwed me out of a lot of the money I should have got by way of settlement.'

'Do you mind if I ask the reason for the divorce? Did your husband find someone else?'

'No, he didn't have the balls to do something like that. In a way, I would have preferred it if he had. No, the divorce was on the grounds of his "unreasonable behaviour".'

'That could cover a great variety of things.'

'It certainly could. And if you think I'm about to itemize them, you've got another think coming. So, given the circumstances that made me end up here, are you telling me I should be sentimental about Polly's Cake Shop? It's never been more than a means to an end. That end is funding my retirement. I'm shortly to retire and my only concern is to get as much money for the place as I can.'

'Are you planning to move away from Fethering?'

'You bet your life I am. The moment I see this village for the last time cannot come soon enough.'

'Right.' A lot of the supplementary questions that Jude had been planning now seemed to be irrelevant. Having heard Josie's views on Fethering, it was clearly not the moment to ask whether she felt a sense of community about the place. (She had a feeling that Josie's views on 'community' would make Carole's sound positively benign.) Nor was it time to enquire whether, as suggested by Flora Claire, she might consider selling Polly's Cake Shop at a lower price 'for the sake of Fethering'. The important part of the interview with Josie Achter could be reckoned to have come to an end.

And she didn't seem the kind of woman who'd appreciate small talk. Jude was preparing the right kind of farewell remarks when footsteps were heard hurrying up from the café and the door opened to admit a short slender girl with wiry dark brown hair, dressed in jeans and T-shirt but carrying a black waitress's uniform. Jude thought there was a pretty strong chance that she was Josie's daughter Rosalie.

'Morning,' said the girl on the way through the sitting room to the rest of the flat.

Josie did not even acknowledge the greeting, and certainly didn't make any introductions. She just called out, 'Ros, I've asked you not to change up here. You don't live here any more. You can change down in the Ladies like the rest of the staff.'

There was no response from the bedroom.

'Your daughter?' asked Jude just for confirmation.

'Yes.' No further comment or elaboration.

'I heard a rumour that at one stage there was a thought of her taking over the business.'

'As I said, there are a lot of rumours in Fethering. Doesn't necessarily mean any of them are true.'

At this point Rosalie, now in waitress kit, came hurrying back through the sitting room. She wasn't carrying her street clothes, so presumably would be returning to the flat to change back at the end of her shift. But as she made her way to the door leading down to the café, neither she nor Josie said anything.

Jude, whose work had often involved her in the complexities of mother-and-daughter relationships, knew that there could be many explanations – including her own presence – for their silence.

But she thought it was worth continuing the previous conversation. 'I'd heard that Rosalie did a Hospitality and Catering course in Brighton.'

'So?'

'Some people thought that was with a view to her taking over the business.'

'Well, some people, not for the first time, were wrong.'

Jude thought she must make one more attempt to fulfil her brief from the SPCS Action Committee. 'From what you said earlier,

Josie, you don't seem to have much sentimental attachment to Fethering . . .?'

'I'm glad I made my attitude clear.'

'Is there any particular reason for your disillusionment?'

'Other than the fact that the place is full of stuck-up bitches?'

'Yes, I admit the village does have its fair share. But, putting that on one side—'

'Fairly hard to put on one side, given that it's the predominant feature of the place.'

'Yes, but on the other hand—'

'Jude, I have run Polly's Cake Shop and I have lived in this flat for over ten years. I have smiled winsomely at the stuck-up bitches of Fethering as I have served them endless pots of tea and cinnamon toast and éclairs. And have any of them ever shown any interest in becoming friends with me? That was in fact a rhetorical question. Not one. In all the time I've been here, I have not been invited to a single person's house. So why should I feel any sentimental attachment to this breeding ground of snobbery?'

'And you think that's the reason why you've been kind of . . . socially excluded? Because the stuck-up bitches regard someone who runs a café as their inferior? Like you're "trade"? Well, I know this village is old-fashioned, but I can assure you that there are a lot of people in Fethering who don't—'

'It's not to do with my being "trade". Or at least, it's only partly that. No, the reason why I'm, as you put it, "socially excluded" is pure, old-fashioned anti-Semitism.'

Jude was knocked sideways by that; the last thing she'd expected to hear. It hadn't occurred to her that Josie Achter was Jewish.

'Oh, it's very subtle in a place like this,' the café owner went on. 'No overt discrimination, no shattered windows, no spray-painting on the walls; just a genteel assumption that just being a Gentile puts you in a superior position to anyone Jewish.'

'Since I've been in Fethering I haven't been aware of any—'

'No, I'm sure you haven't, and that's because you're not Jewish. You don't hear the sniggers and the mumblings about the "chosen race" and "buckles".'

'Sorry?'

'Rhyming slang. "Buckle my shoe – Jew." Haven't you heard it?'

'No.'

'You would have done if you were Jewish,' said Josie bitterly. 'Well, I've had to put up with that all my life. I thought maybe I'd put it behind me when I "married out", but no, my bastard ex-husband turned out to have his own private brand of anti-Semitism. 'And it's not just me who's suffered. Rosalie, my daughter, has had to put up with the same thing over the years. In her teens she joined the local tennis club and the Fethering Yacht Club – she used to be quite handy in boats. But I had to take her out of both clubs because of the way she was insulted there.'

'Are you sure you weren't—?'

'If you're about to say: am I sure I was not being hypersensitive – no, I was not!'

Jude, who had been about to say something on those lines, kept quiet as Josie Achter continued, 'This country, England, so proud of its human-rights record, the diversity of its population, is still riddled with anti-Semitism. And it's at its worst in a "nice, middle-class" area like Fethering.

'So no, I don't feel any sentimental attraction to the place. When I sell up, I'm going to move to Hove, where at least there is a substantial Jewish community, where we can gather together for self-protection.

'I don't know the precise reason for you setting up this meeting, Jude, but if it was in the hope that I might be ready to co-operate with your precious "action committee", forget it. Also, don't attempt to contact me again. If you ask to see me, I will refuse to see you. And, since everyone in this place has already categorized me as the hard-bitten grasping Jewess, then I'm going to live up to that stereo-type. My only concern about Polly's Cake Shop is that I sell it as soon as I can and that I get as much money for it as is humanly possible. I have no interest in what happens to the place after I move out.'

SEVEN

Carole was back at High Tor that Friday evening. Gaby had been checked over at the hospital in every possible way and passed as going through a normal pregnancy. But the sudden summons from Stephen, and the stay in Fulham, had unsettled her mother-in-law. They had reminded her of the potential perils of childbirth, and Carole knew she would not relax again (even to the small extent that she ever did) until the baby had safely arrived.

Jude was spending the weekend leading healing workshops at a Wellbeing Festival in Hastings so, apart from a quick handover of Gulliver on the Friday evening, the two women did not spend much time together. Though Carole was aware that Jude had attended the SPCS Action Committee on the Wednesday, she did not know that her neighbour had ended up being voted on to it. Nor that she had been delegated to talk to Josie Achter.

And because of the strict client confidentiality rules that Jude imposed on herself, she had not mentioned to Carole anything about Sara Courtney's real – or perhaps hallucinatory – sighting of a dead body at Polly's Cake Shop.

The second meeting of the SPCS Action Committee at Hiawatha, a fortnight after the first, was a smaller affair because only those who had been voted on were invited. Phoebe Braithwaite, who hadn't been elected (her husband had been worried about opening himself up to charges of nepotism – or perhaps uxorism), lurked in the kitchen. The door was half open, so that she could in fact hear all of the committee's proceedings – but more importantly be instantly ready when the Commodore demanded she produce refreshments for the assembled company.

There was one man sitting at the table who wasn't a committee member, but from the way the Chair venerated him, it was clear that Quintus Braithwaite was very proud of his new social acquisition.

The man was around fifty, toned and tanned, as if he knew how to look after himself. He wore a blue linen suit over a coral-coloured open-necked shirt. On his wrist was a chunky gold watch, which even Jude, who had no interest in such things, could recognize to be very expensive.

Quintus Braithwaite hurried through the necessary early business – Item 1: Apologies (England must surely be the only country in the world where all meetings start with apologies) and Item 2: Signing the Minutes of the Last Meeting. Then, unable to contain himself any longer, he announced: 'I would now like to introduce to you—'

'On a point of order, Mr Chairman . . .' The interruption came, inevitably, from Arnold Bloom.

'Yes?' said the Commodore testily.

'According to the Agenda which was circulated to members – with great efficiency, may I say, by our secretary Wendy Roote – the next item after the signature of the minutes – "Item 3" – is not introducing an outsider to our committee. It is "Matters Arising", meaning "Matters Arising from the Minutes of the Last Meeting".'

'I know what "Matters Arising" means, thank you, Arnold, but I think possibly the gentleman I am about to introduce has more relevance to the work of this committee than any pettifogging adherence to the order of the meeting's Agenda.'

'I'm sorry, Mr Chairman, but if you are describing me as "pettifogging", I must ask you to withdraw the remark.'

'I'm not describing *you* as "pettifogging", I am describing the meeting's *processes* as "pettifogging".'

'But,' Arnold persisted, 'we members of the committee represent the processes of this committee, and to describe those processes as "pettifogging" is tantamount to describing *us* as "pettifogging".'

Commodore Quintus Braithwaite had never had a very long fuse, and Arnold Bloom's arguments were shortening it by the minute. 'Oh, for God's sake!' he burst out.

But the voice of reason that interrupted him came from an unlikely source, the man in the blue linen suit whom he was so keen to introduce. 'Listen,' he said, 'the last thing I want to do is to disrupt the normal business of your committee. Quintus, why don't you go through the rest of the Agenda items in the normal way and then introduce me at the end?'

'Well, because I . . .' But the Commodore could recognize he was being offered a lifeline, and took it. 'Very well.' He looked down at the Agenda. 'I'll introduce you when we get to "Item 8 – Fundraising". That would be appropriate.'

'Sounds fine by me,' said the man in the blue linen suit.

Arnold Bloom sat back comfortably into his Hiawatha armchair, another small victory registered.

Quintus Braithwaite rather grudgingly then went through Items 3 to 8. There were no 'Matters Arising' from the reading of the Minutes which would not be covered under future Agenda items. 'Item 4' was a subject which Arnold Bloom had managed to shoe-horn in – 'Location of Future Meetings'. This was a continuation of the discussion he had initiated at the previous meeting – whether the SPCS Action Committee should continue to meet at Hiawatha or in some other venue. Without actually saying that the Chair might benefit too much from home advantage and some of the weaker committee members might be over-impressed by his lifestyle and hospitality, Arnold did make a strong case for other meeting places to be considered.

Eventually, in the traditional cop-out favoured by all committees, it was decided to appoint a subcommittee to investigate alternative venues.

'Item 5' was 'Publicity and Profile'. Lesley Tarquin immediately produced an iPad mini, to the consternation of some of the older committee members who were still using paper notebooks. 'Well, I assessed the local publicity outlets,' she said. 'I've talked to Vince at the *Fethering Observer* and he's virtually given me carte blanche to put in as much stuff about the SPCS Action Committee as we want to. We've left it that I just send him press releases and he'll print them verbatim. I've contacted the *West Sussex Gazette* and *Sussex Life*, though the latter's a monthly lifestyle magazine and might not be right for us. I've also followed up on local radio and I've got Jezza from FOAM FM virtually eating out of my hand. I've emailed Will at Radio Solent and Flick at Radios Surrey and Sussex, but haven't heard back yet. Same goes for Barry at *South Today* and Fizz at Meridian. And obviously I've been busy on Facebook and Twitter.'

'Obviously,' said Quintus Braithwaite, as if he knew what the hell she was talking about.

'That's it so far,' said Lesley Tarquin, 'but I have made a start.'

There was an impressed silence. Publicity was an area in which all local Fethering societies fell down. However much effort there was put into organizing events, most of them failed because no one knew they were on. To hear someone talking about media outlets with the confidence and professionalism of Lesley Tarquin was unfamiliar to most of those present that evening at Hiawatha.

'Well,' said the Commodore, choosing his words carefully. He was very impressed by Lesley – and also rather attracted to her – but he couldn't quite keep the patronizing tone out of his voice as he continued, 'You've done frightfully well and I'm sure when your contacts are joined up with those I have built up over the years through the Naval Club and Fethering Yacht Club, we could be looking at an excellent media profile for the SPCS Action Committee.'

Lesley Tarquin smiled her satisfaction at this endorsement.

'Anything else you want to add?' asked the Chair.

'No. Not at the moment.'

'Good. Splendid work, Lesley. And we move on to "Item 6" on our Agenda . . .' He glanced down at his papers with disapproval. 'It says "Possible Alternative Uses for Polly's Cake Shop". I person-ally feel that discussion of this kind of thing is premature. We need to get the funding and ownership of the property sorted before we get into this kind of detail. In fact, I'm quite surprised you put it on the Agenda, Wendy.'

But the Secretary wasn't about to stand for public criticism of that kind. 'It was agreed at the last meeting that any elected committee member could put forward items for the Agenda.'

'Yes, but you should have checked it with me first,' came the testy response. 'I could have told you that this was not relevant.'

'You've had the papers for nearly a week,' Wendy Roote defended herself stoutly. 'If you wanted to raise any objection, you had plenty of time to—'

'Well, all right I didn't. But I'm objecting now. We don't have any ownership rights – or indeed any other rights – yet in Polly's Cake Shop, so discussing "Alternative Uses" for it would seem to me to be a complete waste of—'

'No, it's not. It's very necessary. It's very important that everyone on the committee is sharing the same mind-set.' The interrupter, perhaps inevitably, was Flora Claire. Jude felt pretty sure that she was the one who had infiltrated 'Item 6' on to the Agenda as she went on, 'I've been talking to various like-minded friends in Fethering during the last couple of weeks, and there's a strong feeling amongst them that—'

'I don't think you should be discussing committee business with your friends,' the Commodore objected through clenched teeth. 'Even "like-minded" ones. It's important – particularly at our planning stage – that we maintain confidentiality about our plans.'

'But it's an issue of great relevance to the people of Fethering, and my friends are all people of Fethering, so I believe that their views are valuable. And there is a general view in the village that we have a great opportunity here, not just to maintain Polly's Cake Shop as it is, but to broaden the scope of its activities away from the crassly commercial to something more spiritual.'

'"Spiritual"?' echoed Quintus Braithwaite despairingly.

'Yes. Fethering is a place of great spirituality. There have been many independently accredited incidents of paranormal activity in the area – especially in the village of Clapham. And ley lines travel directly from Stonehenge – or "Stone Hinge", as it should be called, because it acts as a *hinge* from which the sun, moon and planets are suspended – right through the centre of Fedborough, which is just up the river from Fethering. Also a lot of psychic phenomena have been recorded in the Chanctonbury Ring area and . . .'

The Commodore tried to cut off this flow of psychobabble, but once again Flora was shown to have a surprising amount of support in the room. Jude kept quiet. She knew that a lot of people in Fethering thought her healing work was at least as bonkers as the stuff Flora was going on about.

It was a good twenty minutes before the Chair managed to end the discussion about Fethering's 'spirituality', and then he only did it by conceding that 'Possible Alternative Uses for Polly's Cake Shop' should appear as an item on the next meeting's Agenda.

He moved on with some relief to 'Item 7: Response from Current Owner of Polly's Cake Shop'.

This didn't take long. It's was Jude's cue to report, and she did so very succinctly, relaying the news that Josie Achter's only interest in her business was how much money she could get for it. And, as for 'Community Spirit', she didn't have any.

Now, finally, Quintus Braithwaite was able to produce his prize exhibit. 'Right, now we come to "Item 8: Fundraising" – and I don't think even you can now object, Arnold' – he smiled viciously at his opponent – 'if I introduce a very important guest.'

He paused for effect, but unfortunately allowed long enough for Arnold Bloom to voice his dissent. 'Well, I think the principle of introducing non-members to a committee meeting without consultation is something that goes against the rules by which this sort of democratic organization should be—'

But the Chair had had enough. Riding roughshod over Arnold, he continued, 'I am very honoured to welcome here Kent Warboys, who is very much a local boy made good. We have met,' he said with some pride, 'through Fethering Yacht Club, of which we are both members, and I'm sure a lot of you present here tonight will know of Kent and his work.

'But for those of you who don't, I should tell you that Kent was brought up right here in Fethering. He attended the local comprehensive school but, in spite of that, still managed to train as an architect. And there are many fine buildings and developments in the Fethering area which are a tribute to Kent's distinctive style.

'In recent years he has moved away from the, as it were, "hands-on" business of architecture towards the bigger challenge of over-seeing major construction projects.'

Again Quintus Braithwaite made the mistake of leaving too long a pause. Arnold Bloom came straight in with: 'You mean he's a property developer?'

'I wouldn't say that, no.' The Chair was well aware that such a description in a place like Fethering was tantamount to an insult. 'I mean, Kent is very aware of both heritage and harmony with the landscape. He's . . . um, he's . . .'

Quintus was in danger of losing it, so the subject of his speech came in to rescue him (and himself).

'If I may speak a little on my own behalf . . .' Kent Warboys' voice, though cultured, had a reassuring undercurrent of local Sussex in it. 'For want of a better description, yes I am a "property developer", but this doesn't necessarily make me the bogie man of the popular press. As Quintus said, my concerns in the work I do are heritage and harmony with the landscape.

'Now those of us down here are fortunate to live in one of the most beautiful parts of England – as a proud Sussex man I'd even say one of the most beautiful parts of the world. I've grown up with that beauty and the last thing I want to do is to spoil it in any way. Projects I've worked on recently – the Smalting Lifeboat Centre and the Clincham Haymarket Gallery—' the mention of these names drew appreciative murmurs from his audience – 'have, I'm glad to say, received very favourable responses and indeed won a few awards for the way they have married contemporary facilities with traditional design.

'You see, I've now got to the stage of my life when, looking back on all the benefits that living in this beautiful area has given me, I'm asking myself: What can I do to pay back some of that good fortune? In what way can I use my skills to give something to the Fethering community? And developing Polly's Cake Shop as a Community Amenity is exactly the sort of project that I think could answer my need. I am proposing that my company, Warboys Heritage Construction, should buy Polly's Cake Shop.'

This raised huge enthusiasm from the committee, even to the extent that Phoebe Braithwaite peered round the kitchen door to see what was going on.

Kent Warboys raised his hands to quell the reaction before it turned into applause. 'Now, I don't want you to think that I'm being completely altruistic here. I'm not proposing to buy that place and make a gift of it to the SPCS Action Committee – much as I would like to be able to do that. No, I am a businessman and what I am proposing is a business plan. If Warboys Heritage Construction were to purchase the Polly's Cake Shop site, my plans would be to improve and refurbish the existing flat above the café, and to build two more flats on what is currently the back yard.'

'But, Kent,' objected Arnold Bloom, gleeful that the conversation had moved on to a subject on which he was something of an expert, 'I think you might find it hard to obtain planning permission for such a project. The local Planning Committee, I'm glad to say, are very averse to uncontrolled development of this locality.'

'Maybe,' Quintus Braithwaite interposed, 'but the members of the Planning Committee are reasonable people. There's one Kent and I know who's also a member of Fethering Yacht Club, and I'm sure if we were to casually spell out to him the advantages of—'

'I'm afraid nowadays backscratching by the Old Boys' Network doesn't work quite the way it used to, Mr Chairman.' Arnold was approaching his high horse with great relish. 'If you're suggesting you're going to get planning permission on a nod and a wink and a few expensive dinners, then—'

'I am not suggesting anything of the kind! I am only saying that if one has useful contacts, one should—'

'And I am telling you that we're no longer in the days of T. Dan Smith and John Poulson!' Puzzled looks on the faces of the younger committee members showed that they weren't familiar with corruption trials of the early 1970s. And also suggested that Arnold Bloom might be a lot older than he looked. He went on, 'Planning permission is not something that can be taken for granted. We're very close here to the Arundel Park Area of Outstanding Natural Beauty, and the idea of luxury flats being built on Fethering seafront is just the kind of thing that . . .'

Kent Warboys had raised a polite finger to stop Arnold in midflow, and it worked. 'I'm sorry to interrupt you, Arnold, but I have no plans to build *luxury* flats. What I am talking of building is what we are constantly being told by every government of every hue is needed – particularly here in the southeast – *affordable housing.*

'The existing flat and the ones I'm proposing to build will be priced in such a way that they could allow three young couples, brought up round here but unable to afford local prices, to stay in the area of their birth.' Another murmur of approbation.

'And in all this, let me stress that I am not forgetting the reason why you are all gathered here tonight at Hiawatha. You are the SPCS Action Committee, and your aim is to meet the goal of saving Polly's Cake Shop. Well, my plans would achieve that, because the profit made on selling the three flats on the site would enable me to offer the ground-floor café area to be developed as a Community Amenity *rent-free!*'

This time Kent Warboys did not prevent the assembled throng from clapping. Nor from strongly endorsing his proposal that Warboys Heritage Construction should enter negotiations for the purchase of Polly's Cake Shop.

Needless to say, the minute Quintus Braithwaite had banged his gavel to mark the official ending of the meeting, Phoebe was straight in from the kitchen with her tray of wine and glasses. There was an atmosphere of celebration in the drinking that followed, and in the course of it Jude was introduced to Kent Warboys.

'Ah, we have a mutual friend,' he said.

'Oh?'

'Sara Courtney.'

'Ah.'

'She's very grateful to you for the help you gave her when—' he didn't want to spell out too much detail in public – 'when she needed it.'

'My pleasure. Glad she's feeling better.'

'Yes,' said Kent Warboys with a grin. 'She's feeling a lot better.'

And the way he said the words made Jude wonder whether he had made any contribution to Sara's newfound well-being.

EIGHT

Jude was surprised the following morning to have a phone call on the dot of seven. It was rather earlier than she liked to begin the process of waking up.

She was also surprised to find that the caller was Carole.

'Is everything all right? Has the baby started?'

'No, I haven't heard anything from Fulham for three days.' She sounded upset by this lack of communication.

'Well, I'm sure in this case no news is good news. They don't want to ring you until there's something to say.'

'Maybe not.' Carole didn't sound convinced. 'Stephen always did have a very secretive streak.'

Congenital? Jude wondered. But she didn't voice the thought. Instead she said, 'Everything will be absolutely fine. Gaby had all those tests last week and they all proved that the baby was in excellent form.'

'Yes. But I still worry.' This was unusual from Carole. Normally she'd do anything rather than express her feelings – or admit to having any. 'I've been awake most of the night.'

Jude was well practised in supplying comfort to the troubled, but she'd rarely had to offer it to her neighbour. 'Look, do you want to come round and talk about it?'

'Well . . .' Carole was tempted. 'But I haven't taken Gulliver out for his walk yet.'

'Or had breakfast?'

'No.'

'Then I'll tell you what we'll do. Just give me time to have a shower and get some clothes on, then I'll join you for a walk. A good workout for Gulliver should take what . . . half an hour . . .?'

'About that.'

'Which would mean that at eight o'clock, when Polly's Cake Shop opens, we could settle down for an indulgently large breakfast there.'

Carole didn't demur. Which was a measure of how bad a state

she was in. Normally she hated being organized by anyone. But on this occasion she needed help. Even more remarkable, she had virtually admitted to Jude that she needed help.

It was nippy on Fethering Beach. The October mornings were cold. Jude had already put Woodside Cottage's central heating on, timed for a couple of hours early morning and a couple early evening. And if she was at home in the evening, she lit a fire. Carole, who still thought the whole concept of central heating was something of an indulgence, hadn't switched hers on yet.

As they passed over the dunes on to the beach, Jude looked back at the service road and the gates to Polly's Cake Shop's yard. Yes, there would be room for a couple of flats there. Not very big, but with amazing views. She looked along the row of similar yards for the other shops and wondered if any of them might be bought up for similar development. And indeed if that was part of Kent Warboys' long-term plan.

But she wasn't there for that kind of speculation. The purpose of the walk was to comfort Carole. 'It's natural for you to worry,' she said, 'but it will all be all right. Because of the tests she had last week you know more about the health of Gaby's than you do about most unborn babies. And it's not as if she had any problems with Lily's birth, did she?'

'Well, the labour wasn't particularly comfortable.'

'No, but it never is. That's why it's called "labour".' Though childless herself, through her clients Jude had a wide knowledge of the problems of pregnancy. 'But is there any particular reason why you're worrying so much about Gaby?'

'Why? Should there be?'

'I don't know, do I? That's why I'm asking. I just wondered if there was anything from your own experience of childbirth that might make you especially anxious.'

'Well . . .'

'What?'

But if Carole had been on the verge of some confession, she changed her mind. 'Nothing,' she replied briskly. 'As you say, labour is never a walk in the park, but with Stephen . . . nothing went wrong.' And that was all Jude was going to get on the subject.

It was quite cold on the beach. The clocks were due to go back the next weekend, but till then it was still dark at seven thirty in the morning. There was also a bit of sea mist. The tide was going out, exposing vast expanses of sand. Unsurprisingly the two women seemed to be alone on the beach, apart from Gulliver, who'd been released from his lead and was conducting elaborate guerrilla warfare with inanimate lumps of seaweed along the shoreline.

'Anyway, how was your *new* committee meeting last night?' Carole asked, infusing the 'new' with the implication that the subject was somehow frivolous and flaky.

'Oh, like committees always are. Tedious and unnecessary.'

'They don't have to be.' During her time at the Home Office, Carole had prided herself on 'running a good committee'. 'It's all a matter of who's chairing the thing. If the Chair's weak, then nothing works.'

'I don't think this Chair's weak so much as self-aggrandizing. Former naval man, pillar of the Fethering Yacht Club, who goes under the unlikely name of Quintus Braithwaite. Have you come across him?' Carole had, after all, been a Fethering resident longer than Jude had.

'Doesn't ring a bell – and it's not the kind of name you'd be likely to forget. Where does he live?'

'The Shorelands Estate.'

Carole let out a snort of contempt. 'Say no more. That lot never leave their gated compound, except to take their 4x4s out to Waitrose. Anyway, you say he's not a weak Chair?'

'No, but he seems to think it's all about him.'

'Oh yes.' Carole nodded sagely. 'That type can be almost as destructive as the weak ones. And this palaver is all in the cause of saving Polly's Cake Shop for the village, is that right?'

'Yes.'

'I can't understand why you got on the committee.'

'Well, it was through a . . .' Jude had nearly said 'friend', but she knew how shirty Carole could get when friends she didn't know about were mentioned '. . . a client.'

'Oh?' Even with the change of word, Carole sounded a bit frosty.

'Yes, she's going through a bad patch; she needs a lot of support.'

'Huh,' said Carole Seddon, as only Carole Seddon could say 'Huh'. 'I thought you gave your patients support by healing them, not by joining committees you don't want to be on.'

Jude knew that the use of the word 'patients' rather than 'clients' was deliberate, an attempt to rile her. She was determined not to react.

But they were interrupted by furious barking from Gulliver. He was over at the shoreline, suspicious and angry, circling something he had found there.

Carole and Jude drew closer. The darkness of the night was paling into grey and they could see quite clearly what had upset the dog.

It was the body of a man, swollen to the point of bursting out of his clothes and hideously discoloured. Ropes tied around his ankles were broken and frayed.

But they could see clearly enough that in his right temple there was a bullet hole.

NINE

'Well,' said Ted Crisp as the two women sat down in the Crown and Anchor with large Sauvignon Blancs that evening, 'it sounds odd to me. Probably means the body wasn't a "Fethering Floater".'

'Oh, I've heard of them, "Fethering Floaters",' said Jude. 'But I can't remember the details.'

'I can remember them,' said Carole tartly. 'The subject came up when that poor boy Aaron Spalding drowned in the Fether.' She was referring to the first case they had ever worked on together, just after Jude had moved into Woodside Cottage.

'Yes. Remind me.'

Ted picked up the cue. 'It's an old tradition round here, a story passed down the generations. But perhaps more believable than many of the Fethering old wives' tales. It's something to do with the Fether being a tidal river and how that affects the currents where it actually meets the English Channel. Basically it's reckoned that anyone who drowns in the Fether gets swept out to sea and then the undertow gets hold of the body and drags it back to land. So they usually turn up on Fethering Beach within twenty-four hours. And they're called the "Fethering Floaters".'

'Well, the one we found this morning wasn't one of them,' Carole observed.

'More likely washed in from the Channel,' said Ted. 'Illegal immigrant, perhaps, trying to get over here in a boat that wasn't seaworthy.' Of course he didn't know anything about the bullet hole.

'Perhaps,' said Carole. 'All I know is that from the state of decomposition, the body had been in the water for considerably longer than twenty-four hours.'

'Yes, it had probably been in there nearer three weeks.' As soon as the words were out, the look on Carole's face told Jude that she shouldn't have said that. She hadn't mentioned anything to her neighbour about Sara Courtney's story of having seen a dead body at Polly's Cake Shop.

'What do you mean by that?' came the instant, suspicious response.

'I just . . . erm . . .' Jude floundered. 'As you say, the state of decomposition. That body looked as if it had been in the sea getting on for three weeks.'

'And since when have you been an expert in forensic pathology, Jude?'

'Oh, you know, you see things. All those grisly American series . . . *CSI* whatever . . . you pick it up.'

Jude knew how unconvincing she sounded. She knew too that, when they were next alone together, Carole would grill her about her lapse. She looked down at her glass, which had unaccountably become empty.

'I think we'd better have a couple more of the large Sauvignon Blancs,' she said to Ted. 'Need it after what we've been through today.'

Carole's instinct to protest that she didn't need any more was stopped at source by Ted actually pouring the drinks. 'Police give you a rough time, did they?' he asked.

'They were studiously polite,' Jude replied. 'But obviously they wanted a lot of information.'

'We were, after all, the first people to discover the body,' said Carole. 'So they started off pretty suspicious. But it soon became clear that there was no possible connection between us and the corpse.'

'And we really had nothing to tell them, beyond the fact that we'd found it. But that didn't stop them grilling us for what felt like hours.'

In spite of uneven encounters with the police since she'd left the Home Office, Carole still had an instinct to protect the Force when it came under attack. 'They were just doing their job, Jude. They usually arrive on a crime scene knowing absolutely nothing about what's happened, none of the background. You can't blame them for all the questions.'

'No, I suppose you're right,' Jude agreed grudgingly.

'Anyway, Carole,' said Ted, 'at least you've provided the *Fethering Observer* with another predictable headline.'

'What do you mean?'

'Well, it's always the same thing when a dead body's found in this part of the world, isn't it? The report always begins: "A woman walking her dog . . ." and then goes on to describe the nasties that the woman walking her dog discovered. And this time you and Gulliver have the honour of playing those two central roles.'

'Yes, I suppose we do,' said Carole. She was subdued, feeling the delayed shock of what she and Jude had encountered on Fethering Beach that morning.

'Anyway,' said Ted, 'from my point of view, speaking as landlord of the Crown and Anchor, I'm just glad it happened now rather than at the beginning of the tourist season. Dead bodies are not among the amenities your average punter looks for in a beach holiday.'

'But you've had a good summer, haven't you?'

'You betcha. Zosia and Ed have worked their little socks off.' He referred to his bar manager and chef. 'No, it's been good.' Ted Crisp still hadn't quite come to terms with the fact that the Crown and Anchor, mainly thanks to Zosia's efficiency and Ed Pollack's cooking, had become a success. Having first become a destination pub, it was now sometimes even referred to as a 'gastropub'. Occasionally he felt nostalgia for its former scruffiness.

'Anyway, enough about things washed up on the beach. Let us lighten the mood with a well-chosen joke.' Ted Crisp could never forget for long that – in a former life – he had been a stand-up comic. 'What lies at the bottom of the ocean and twitches?'

'I don't know,' said Jude obediently. 'What *does* lie at the bottom of the ocean and twitches?'

Ted Crisp burst into a raucous laugh as he replied, 'A nervous wreck!'

Carole sniffed. 'You've always known how to raise the tone, haven't you, Ted?'

They ended up staying in the Crown and Anchor to eat. As with the second glass of Sauvignon Blanc, Carole had initially resisted the suggestion, but her mind didn't take much changing. The morning's events had unsettled her and the prospect of fisherman's pie was a comforting one.

But she had hardly taken a mouthful of Ed Pollack's speciality when Carole received a call on her mobile that put dead bodies and everything else clean out of her mind.

It was from Stephen. Gaby had gone into labour.

TEN

She couldn't eat any more and said she had to get back to High Tor in case the phone rang. Jude's argument that if Stephen had contacted her on the mobile once he could do so again did not hold any sway. Carole needed to be alone. Alone with her fears.

She spent a terrible night. She had been nervous when Gaby was in labour with Lily, but the sheer gorgeousness of her granddaughter had dulled and sanitized the memory of that. This time she was paranoid with worry. And she knew why.

She didn't even attempt to go to bed. She knew there was no possibility of sleep. Instead she sat downstairs in her antiseptically clean sitting room, with her mobile on the table next to her landline phone, willing them both to ring. It was a very long night.

Gulliver, sensing her distress, sat by her feet, seeming to wish there was something he could bring her by way of comfort. But there wasn't anything.

Eventually, at six in the morning, Carole willed herself to have a shower and change into fresh clothes. She wondered whether she should pack a bag in readiness for a summons to Fulham, but no. That would be tempting providence.

In such a bad state was she that, for the second morning running, Carole found herself ringing Woodside Cottage on the dot of seven.

'Any news?' Jude immediately asked.

'Nothing,' Carole replied desolately. 'I was thinking I should take Gulliver out for his walk, but I don't want to leave the house.'

'You've got your mobile,' Jude reassured her, 'and the signal on Fethering Beach is pretty good.'

'Yes.' There was an empty silence. 'You wouldn't mind taking him, would you, Jude?'

'No, that's fine. Just give me time to get some clothes on and I'll be right round.'

*   *   *

They sat in the hygienic anonymity of Carole's kitchen. She had offered coffee in a knee-jerk hospitable gesture and been a little surprised when Jude said yes. All her neighbour had needed to do was to pick up Gulliver and take him down to Fethering Beach. But Gulliver had decided that wasn't about to happen straight away and snuggled down into his usual place beside the Aga.

Once they were both sitting at the table with coffee cups, Carole was surprised to find she was comforted. She felt so vulnerable that Jude's presence was infinitely reassuring.

'What is the matter?' her neighbour asked.

'My daughter-in-law's in labour. That's what's the matter. You know that.'

'Yes, but that doesn't justify the state you're in, Carole.'

'I don't know what you mean.'

'I think you do. Look, I know you pretty well by now.' Carole didn't like that idea of anyone knowing her 'pretty well', but she still found perverse comfort in Jude's words. 'And I know you keep a tight control on your emotions. But right now you're in a really bad way.'

'Maybe.' It was more than Carole would usually admit.

'Is it because it's the second baby?'

Carole looked at her neighbour sharply. 'How do you know that?'

'I don't know.' Jude wasn't about to claim any psychic powers. She knew the contemptuous reaction she'd get to anything of that kind. 'It just seemed, the state you've been in the last few months, compared to how you were during Gaby's first pregnancy.'

'I didn't realize it showed so much.'

'It did. It does.'

There was a silence. Then, slowly, Carole said, 'If you really want to know . . .'

'I'm not pushing you. If you'd rather not talk about it . . .'

But Carole was under way and not to be deflected. Her voice sounded very even as she made the confession. 'After Stephen was born, a couple of years after I did get pregnant again. The baby went to term and was stillborn. It was a girl. I felt very guilty.'

'But it wasn't your fault. Just incredibly bad luck.'

'Not guilty towards the baby. I felt guilty for the effect it had on Stephen. I became very withdrawn from everything after it happened. Withdrawn from Stephen. Withdrawn from David. I think that's probably what ended the marriage. Neither of us could talk about it, talk about her. We just drew further apart.'

Carole wasn't the kind of woman to cry, but Jude had no doubt about the level of emotion she was experiencing. She also knew that her neighbour would probably later regret how much she was opening up. She would feel embarrassed and never want the subject mentioned again. Jude was prepared for that. If her neighbour never again referred to this conversation, she would never raise it.

Jude reached across the table and put her hand on Carole's. It flinched momentarily, but then let the hand stay there. Between the two women silence reigned.

It was broken by the ringing of the landline. Stephen announced that Gaby had just given birth to another girl. Mother and baby were both doing fine. She was going to be called Chloe 'with no dots on the "e" – we don't want to make life difficult for her when she gets to school.'

ELEVEN

Saturday morning was a very busy time at Polly's Cake Shop. Though the bulk of its business came from tourists and day-trippers, Saturday morning was for the locals. The village residents these days did most of their major shopping at Sainsbury's in Rustington or Waitrose in Littlehampton, but this was the day when they patronized the shops along Fethering Parade (including the uniquely inefficient supermarket Allinstore). Saturday morning was also the time when the working population of the village would gather in Polly's for coffee and gossip. And weekenders from London would also muscle in, giving themselves the illusion that they were part of country life.

Unsurprisingly, the gossip that particular morning hinged largely on the body that had been discovered on the Thursday on Fethering Beach.

Carole was in Fulham, getting to know her junior granddaughter Chloe and ensuring that the nose of Lily, the senior one, was not put too much out of joint. So when Jude entered Polly's Cake Shop for a cappuccino and a guilt-free éclair, she was surprised to find herself something of a celebrity as 'one of the people who found the body'.

Sara Courtney saw her come in and took her order. And it was a more cheerful and bouncier Sara Courtney than Jude had seen for a while. On the previous Wednesday at Hiawatha Sara had seemed tense and a little paranoid. Now she looked more relaxed and as a result a lot prettier. And Jude could tell the change was not just the professional smiling front she put on in her working role as waitress.

'All right?' she asked.

'Good, thanks. Cappuccino and éclair?'

'Predictable, aren't I?'

'Not in everything, Jude.' And with a grin Sara went off to fetch her order.

Jude quickly decided that the woman couldn't yet have made any connection between the body found on Fethering Beach and the one she had (or hadn't) seen in the store room at Polly's. None of the news bulletins had yet mentioned the bullet hole in the man's temple.

Jude slowly looked around the café, giving small smiles to people she recognized. Most Fethering residents knew all the other Fethering residents by sight. They also, even if they had never spoken, knew their names, their domestic circumstances and their secrets. Village gossip had never let respect for accuracy interrupt its flow.

Jude was quite surprised to see that Phoebe Braithwaite was sitting at a table adjacent to hers. And it was a very voluble Phoebe Braithwaite, unlike the cowed, twittery figure on the fringes of the committee meeting at Hiawatha. She was clearly a woman who blossomed once she was moved out of her husband's shadow.

Phoebe, like the others at her table, was dressed in immaculate leisurewear. White jeans and pale blue deck shoes, a neatly cut blazer over a horizontally striped top. The image was casual and nautical, but the perfection and obvious expense of her ensemble produced an effect which was far from relaxed. Phoebe Braithwaite wasn't the kind of woman who possessed clothes to slop around in.

Her blonded hair was flawlessly cut, suggesting she had just emerged from an appointment at Marnie's Hair Salon along the Parade.

And in the hive of her table, she was clearly the queen bee. She led the conversation and Jude's arrival had given her another opportunity to assert her dominance. 'We were just talking about the terrible discovery on the beach on Thursday . . .'

'Oh yes.'

'And you, I gather, were one of the people who had the misfortune to find the body . . .?' Jude admitted that this was indeed the case. 'Oh, you poor thing. How dreadful for you. Incidentally, I don't think we all know each other. This is Jude and this is . . .'

Phoebe proceeded to introduce the other five women around her table. They were all dressed in similarly unrelaxed leisurewear and looked as if they too had just come out of Marnie's. They all had names in the Joanna/Samantha range which Jude didn't really take in.

'Well, as you can imagine,' Phoebe went on, 'there's been all kinds of theories around Fethering as to who the man was and how he got there.'

'I'm not at all surprised. Fethering has the capacity to get extremely aerated about much less than a dead body.'

'So true, Jude, so true. But tell me . . .' As introducer of 'one of the people who found the body', Phoebe Braithwaite was going to take full advantage of her privileged position. 'Have you got any thoughts as to who the deceased might be?'

'None at all, I'm afraid. I'd certainly never seen him before.'

'I think he was probably an illegal immigrant, fell off a leaky boat,' suggested one of the women called Joanna or Samantha.

'Well, I too think he was an illegal immigrant, but I don't think he fell out of a boat. He fell out of the wheel housing of an aeroplane when the wheels were lowered prior to landing at Gatwick,' said another Joanna or Samantha.

'I'm absolutely certain,' a third Joanna or Samantha interposed, 'that he's a victim of gang wars in Brighton. There's a big turf battle over drugs going on and people they don't like either get shot or get put in what they call a "concrete overcoat" and dropped into—'

But Phoebe Braithwaite had been upstaged for far too long. She came in forcefully, saying, 'I think in these circumstances one should consult an expert, someone who knows about the ways of the sea. And I am fortunate to be married to just such an expert. As I'm sure most of you know, Quintus is a Commodore and he spent his entire career in the Royal Navy. So when he expresses a view on something like this, one can assume he knows what he's talking about. And his view about the body found on Fethering Beach is—'

'Sorry to interrupt you,' said a voice containing no hint of apology, 'but here's your cappuccino and éclair, Jude love.'

It was the tall waitress Binnie, looking only marginally less eccentric in her black and white uniform than she had in her street clothes when Jude had last seen her. Her grey hair was still stretched back into a ballerina bun.

'Oh, thanks, Binnie.'

'Apologies for the waitress transplant. Young madam who took your order is busy chatting someone up on her mobile.'

'Chatting someone up? Who is she—?'

But Binnie's mind had moved on. 'Talking about the body, were you?'

'Well, these ladies were,' said Jude.

'I bet he was local.' Binnie delivered her opinion in a manner that suggested it was the only possible view. 'Dogs return to their own vomit.' And with that gnomic utterance she made her way back to the kitchen.

There was a moment of bemused silence before one of the Joannas or Samanthas said, 'All right, Phoebe, so what does Quintus say about the body?' There was a note of resentment in her voice, as if the woman had already heard quite enough of Phoebe's husband's pontifications on a wide range of subjects.

But his wife was quite ready, even eager, to relay another one. 'Well, he's very sorry that he's not been able to see the body first hand, because he'd be in a much better position to give an accurate assessment if he had. He's seen a lot of casualties from naval accidents over the years. But Quintus's view is that, because of the way the tides work around Fethering – which he knows well as an experienced yachtsman in these waters – the body could not have come from our side of the Channel.'

'Sorry, what do you mean?' asked one of the Joannas or Samanthas.

'Quintus is convinced that the man didn't enter the water from anywhere along the south coast. In other words, whoever had the daft idea about him being the victim of gang warfare in Brighton, well, that just can't be right.' The Joanna or Samantha in question pursed her lips. 'Quintus thinks the man either entered the sea from the North Coast of France or fell off a vessel in the Channel.'

'Exactly what I said!' crowed the relevant Joanna or Samantha. 'He's an illegal immigrant who fell off a leaky boat! You know, these people smugglers who charge them thousands of pounds to travel in vessels that aren't seaworthy, they're terrible people. They're murderers and they just don't care. I read about them in the *Daily Mail*.'

So that must be right, thought Jude ironically. But Phoebe Braithwaite had resented the Joanna or Samantha's interruption, because she hadn't yet finished repeating her husband's views on the body found on Fethering Beach. (Which also of course must be right, thought Jude ironically.)

'Quintus says the most likely thing is that the body was that of a Russian sailor whose ship had called in to some port in Northern France – like Dieppe or Boulogne, let's say. He says there are a lot of Russian seamen in every kind of commercial vessels these days.

And Quintus is pretty sure that this "poor bastard" – his words, not mine, I hasten to add . . .' She tittered at her daring. '. . . Anyway, he'd gone on shore leave and got a skinful of booze and missed his footing on the way back to his vessel and drowned there, and then the currents carried him out into the Channel and deposited him on Fethering Beach.'

'So Quintus reckoned he drowned?' asked Jude.

'Well, of course, yes. What other possibility is there?'

Jude thought it was probably just as well that the assembled ladies in Polly's Cake Shop didn't know about the bullet hole she had seen in the man's temple.

And the bullet hole which Sara Courtney had seen earlier actually inside Polly's Cake Shop. Assuming, of course, that Sara Courtney had seen anything.

Which, in spite of the woman's denials, Jude now felt certain she had.

She also felt certain that before too long the investigating police would make public the fact that the man had been shot. And she wondered what fresh theories that news would generate among the Joannas or Samanthas of Fethering.

TWELVE

Jude woke up on the Sunday morning and switched on Radio Four. She wasn't a regular listener to the channel, but now awaited in every bulletin something about the Fethering Beach body. She was rather confused to find that she wasn't hearing the regular news programme, and took a moment to realize that British summertime had ended and she'd gained an hour during the night.

Jude also woke up with something of a dilemma. She hadn't seen Sara Courtney again after the woman had taken her order in Polly's Cake Shop the previous morning. Presumably she'd been busy in the kitchen. Anyway, even if they had met again, the café was a rather public arena in which to have the kind of conversation Jude needed to have with Sara.

It was because she knew about the woman's fragility that she felt the conversation just had to take place. So far Sara hadn't apparently made any connection between the body she saw (or hallucinated) and the one found the previous Thursday on Fethering Beach. But it was only a matter of time before the news emerged that the man had been shot rather than drowned. The information would probably be revealed in a police news conference and then spread around all of the media. It'd be front-page news in the *Fethering Observer*. There was no way Sara could avoid knowing about it.

And, given the woman's previous history, Jude was worried about the effect the revelation would have on her. If the case of the Fethering Beach body became a murder inquiry, Sara Courtney would either have to become involved or live in fear of being investigated.

So Jude wanted to talk to her, fill her in on what was likely to happen, to cushion the prospective blow.

But that Sunday morning there was no reply from either her landline or her mobile. Jude left messages on both, asking Sara to ring back but not giving any clue as to why she wanted to talk.

Jude got up in a leisurely fashion and had a long bath, laced with essential oils, while incense burned around her.

She was surprised how much she wanted to talk to Carole, to share with her speculation about the body they had discovered. But she'd heard nothing since her neighbour had set off for Fulham on the Friday morning. Jude could have rung the mobile, but didn't want to intrude on the euphoria and anxiety of Chloe's arrival. Carole would communicate in her own good time.

So, relaxed by her bath and still feeling self-indulgent, Jude decided that she would treat herself to lunch at the Crown and Anchor. Having picked up a copy of the *Mail on Sunday* (really just to make her cross), she arrived on the dot of twelve, just as the pig-tailed blond bar manager Zosia was unlocking the door for Sunday opening.

The Polish girl enveloped her in a huge hug. Zosia had adored both of them ever since Jude and Carole had investigated the death of her brother Tadeusz. Had Carole been there, she too would have received a huge hug, which would have pleased and embarrassed her in equal measure.

Zosia went straight behind the bar and, without asking for the order, poured a large glass of New Zealand Sauvignon Blanc. 'If you're lunching, Ed's Sunday Special is a cassoulet. And we've got all the usual joints as well.'

'Cassoulet sounds wonderful. Real winter warmer. Funny how the clocks changing always makes you feel that winter's on the way.'

'Would you like me to put your order through straight away?'

'I'm not in a hurry, Zosia.'

'Well, look, shall I put it through in half an hour? I only say that because we've got a big family party booked in at twelve thirty. Might be wise to get your order in before the kitchen gets really busy.'

'Good thinking. Yes, if you could put it through in half an hour, that'd be great. Thus giving me half an hour's drinking time to get really cross with the *Mail on Sunday*.'

'I hadn't got you down as a *Mail on Sunday* reader, Jude.' Ted Crisp had appeared from the kitchen door. His faded summer T-shirt had given way to a faded sweatshirt, perhaps another homage to the ending of British Summer Time. Winter was definitely on its way.

'I like to vary my reading occasionally,' said Jude. 'See how the other half thinks.'

'I see. Now if it had been Carole reading the *Mail on Sunday*, I wouldn't have thought anything odd about that. She sounds like she's quoting from it every time she opens her mouth.'

'Now that's unfair, Ted.'

'Only slightly.' He grinned behind his scruffy beard. 'You have to admit Carole's opinionated, don't you?'

'I'll give you that.' Jude grinned back, not for the first time amazed to recall that Ted and Carole had once had an affair. Inevitably it hadn't lasted very long, but there was still a tenderness between the two of them. 'Anyway, big news on the Carole front is that she has just become a grandmother for the second time.'

'Oh, great. What was it? A baby?' Ted Crisp could never quite escape his past as a stand-up.

'Ha. Ha. Very funny. Little girl called Chloe. Born Friday morning. Carole's up in Fulham with them now.'

'Oh well, do pass on my congratulations to her.'

'Course I will.'

Ted looked around the bar. There were very few customers. 'The good burghers of Fethering haven't got used to the time change yet.'

'No.'

He leant forward conspiratorially against the bar. 'What about this body you two found then? Any more information?'

Jude shook her head. 'Not a squeak. Police seem to be playing things very close to their chest.'

'Presumably that forensic stuff takes time. Identifying the poor sod, checking his DNA, all that malarkey.'

'Probably.'

'Hm.' The landlord shrugged. 'Oh well. Basic thing is, he's dead and we're still alive.'

'That's a very philosophical thought, Ted.'

'Yes. I do have my introspective moments, you know.' He looked very gloomy. 'So we should continue to enjoy everything life brings us, shouldn't we?'

'Sounds like the best approach, yes.' Jude changed tack. Ted Crisp, from all the people he encountered and conversations he heard over the bar was a useful source of Fethering information. 'Have you come across a man called Kent Warboys?'

'Architect, property developer? Yes, I know him. He comes in here every now and then.'

'And what do you know about him?'

'What do you mean?'

'"Property developer" can have so many different meanings, can't it? For a lot of people round here it's usually a term of abuse.'

Ted chuckled. 'Take your point. Well, from what I know of him, and what I've heard about him from other people, Kent Warboys is one of the good guys. Yes, he's in the business for the money – and has done very well out of it – but he also seems genuinely to care about the projects he gets involved with. You know, he wants to build stuff that kind of fits the area, not the kind of monstrosities you see all along the coast here. You should have a look at his own place.'

'Where's that?'

'Right here in Fethering. Other side of the Fether estuary, opposite the yacht club. He converted a bunch of old fishermen's huts. Won an award for it, I think, you know, for sympathetic, environmentally friendly conversion. All that bloody Green nonsense.' He looked directly into Jude's eyes. 'I gather he's got an interest in developing Polly's Cake Shop.'

'News travels fast.'

'Surely you've been in Fethering long enough not to be surprised by that?'

'True.'

'Kent was in here on Wednesday night.'

'Was he?' Jude thought back. He must have gone to the Crown and Anchor after the SPCS Action Committee meeting at Hiawatha.

'And he seemed to have got a new girlfriend.'

'Oh?'

'All over her he was . . . well, they was all over each other. And he was showing off in that way that men only do right at the beginning of a relationship. Before they start taking the woman for granted. Know what I mean?'

Oh yes. Jude knew exactly what he meant. 'Did you recognize the woman?'

'Sure did. I've forgotten her name but I'd recognize it if someone said it. Spanish looking, she is. Works as a waitress in Polly's.'

'Sara Courtney?'

'That's the one.'

Jude felt rather pleased to have confirmed the suspicion that had been born when she talked to Kent Warboys after the last SPCS Action Committee meeting at Hiawatha.

By the time Jude's cassoulet had arrived, the Crown and Anchor was very full. Sunday lunch was one of its busiest times and she was glad she'd taken Zosia's advice about ordering before the rush. She felt very mellow working her way through Ed Pollack's winter warmer and down her second large New Zealand Sauvignon Blanc. And the bigotry of the *Mail on Sunday* was keeping her at a pleasant level of simmering irritation.

A text arrived on her mobile. She was surprised to see it was from Carole. Not surprised that her neighbour was contacting her, but that she should be using the medium of text. Carole was always slow to take on new technology (though once she had taken it on, she became almost obsessively enthusiastic about it – that had certainly been the case with her laptop).

The message simply said that she had arrived back at High Tor and wondered where Jude was. A quick call brought her down to the Crown and Anchor, where she accepted Jude's offer of a large Sauvignon Blanc 'to wet the baby's head'. She also followed her neighbour's recommendation and ordered the cassoulet.

Jude wanted to get straight down to talking about the Fethering Beach body, but knew she had to ask first about the new arrival. And she found Carole in a rare state of ecstasy verging on the poetic when she talked about her new granddaughter. Chloe was the most beautiful creature who had ever been born, totally unlike her sister in appearance but retaining that baby's ability to look like both of her parents (just as Lily had done). And equally beautiful.

Lily, incidentally, was being extraordinarily good about the new arrival, positively welcoming. Absolutely no signs of jealousy yet, though Carole did concede that it was early days in the relationship between the two.

Then, to Jude's amazement, Carole pulled out her phone to show her some photographs of the new arrival. The amazement arose not from the fact that photographs had been taken, but that they had been taken on a phone. Though it had other capacities, Carole had always regarded her mobile as a device for the making and receiving of phone calls, differing from a landline receiver only in its portability. And suddenly, within two days, she had started using it to send text messages and to take photographs. Jude wondered what had caused the change.

Though she had never had children of her own, and did not feel the lack of them in her life, Jude was not immune to the enchantments of the young, and cooed appropriately at the pictures she was shown. Chloe Seddon looked to be a perfect newborn baby and, like many newborn babies, seemed resolutely unwilling to open her eyes, especially when being rather cautiously cuddled by her older sister. There was even a photograph of Chloe being tentatively held by her grandmother. The whole family looked relieved and happy, and on the face of Gaby was an expression of exhausted triumph.

Jude did not wish to appear uninterested by moving the conversation on, but fortunately Carole herself changed the subject. 'Anyway, what with all that's been going on, I haven't seen much news for the last couple of days. Listened to Radio Four when I was driving down from Fulham this morning, but there was nothing about the Fethering body. Have I missed anything?'

'I'm afraid not. Total news blackout on the subject from official sources . . . though, needless to say, there's been a lot of unbridled local speculation.'

'Yes, I bet there has. Any of it worth listening to?'

'Well, the trouble is, as ever in Fethering, a large number of theories are being put forward, but none of them is based on any solid facts at all.'

'Sounds familiar. And have the police been in touch with you again?' Jude shook her head. 'No, nor me. I kept checking my mobile for messages, but there was nothing. Nothing on my answering machine at High Tor either.'

'But, so far as we know, the police are continuing to conduct their investigations?'

'One would assume so, yes. But, as ever, they're not rushing to share their findings with the amateur sleuths of Fethering.'

'No.' Carole grimaced and then looked sharply at Jude. 'And what have you found out? I'll bet you know more than you did when we last met.'

'Well . . .' Jude was faced with a dilemma; one which she had known would come up at some point. Maintaining the confidentiality of her clients was a strong principle with her, and this was not the first time that principle had been threatened in the course of an investigation.

She tried to think of a way in which she could tell Carole why she thought the mystery man had been murdered, without giving away the secrets which Sara Courtney had confided to her in her professional capacity.

And she reminded herself that when Sara had come to see her a couple of Sundays before, it hadn't actually been in the context of a healing consultation. But to use that fact to justify a breach of confidentiality would, she knew, be mere casuistry. She decided that the only way she could share the information she wanted to with Carole was by not naming names. It might be clumsy, but it would not compromise her principle.

'Listen, there are reasons why I can't give you all the details . . .'

'I see,' said Carole, her nose immediately put out of joint.

Might as well be honest. 'It involves client confidentiality.'

'Oh yes?' There was a particular brand of scepticism that Carole reserved for conversations about her neighbour's work as a healer. Though never voicing the opinion in quite those terms, she secretly thought a lot of what Jude did was 'mumbo-jumbo and psychobabble'.

'The fact is, Carole, I heard from someone—'

'A patient?'

'As you know, I prefer to call them "clients".'

'Oh yes, of course. But it was from a client, was it?' Carole's tone was already implying the unreliability of the source.

'Yes, it was. And she said—'

'A female client then?'

'Yes,' Jude conceded. 'Anyway, I saw her . . . let me think, when was it? Yes, exactly four weeks ago. On the Sunday. And she said she'd seen the dead body of a man . . .'

'Really?'

'. . . with a bullet hole in his temple.'

'Where did she see it?'

'Right here in Fethering.'

'What, on the beach?'

'No.' Jude was realizing how difficult it was going to be to keep her source anonymous under Carole's beady interrogation. 'No, she saw it in Polly's.'

'In Polly's? What, when it was full of people?'

'No, no. After everyone had gone, when she was locking up.'

Carole pounced. 'So she works at Polly's, does she?' Jude could not deny it. 'So we're talking about Sara Courtney, aren't we?'

'Well . . .'

'Don't deny it. How many other clients of yours work at Polly's Cake Shop?'

'Yes, it was her.' Well, she'd tried. And, despite a residue of guilt, Jude felt quite relieved the truth was out. It would make her conversation with Carole a lot easier.

'So where did she see the body?

'In the store room. Well, that is . . . she wasn't absolutely sure whether she'd seen it or not.'

'"Not sure whether she'd seen it"? I think generally speaking, when people see dead bodies, they know whether they've seen them or not.'

'Sara had been very ill.'

'Huh.' Like many people who conduct their lives on the edge of an emotional precipice, Carole Seddon was contemptuous about the concept of mental illness. She went on, 'Was she alone when she saw – or didn't see – the body?'

'Yes.'

'Nobody in the flat upstairs?'

'Apparently not.'

'Was there any sign of a gun in the store room?'

'Yes. Sara said she saw one.'

'Suicide then?'

'Except that the body was lying on the floor, and the gun was on a windowsill, way out of reach of the victim.'

'Murder then,' said Carole.

THIRTEEN

I t was on the Tuesday that the police finally gave a press conference. And identified the body that had been found on Fethering Beach.

His name was Amos Green, aged sixty-four. He was a retired chartered surveyor who was married and lived in Kingston.

The photograph of him shown on the *South Today* coverage of the story was very blurred, a detail blown up from a group picture at a wedding or some other social event. Neither Carole nor Jude could recognize in it the swollen and discoloured face they had seen on Fethering Beach.

The cause of the man's death was not drowning. He had been killed by a gunshot. Police investigations were continuing.

By the time the *Fethering Observer* was published on the Thursday a better photograph had been found. The face that stared out from the front page had very dark eyes, thinning grey hair and a slightly roguish expression.

He apparently had no connection with Fethering. He had lived and worked all his life in Surrey and had been a local councillor in the Kingston area for some years.

The *Fethering Observer* confirmed that he had been shot and that police investigations were continuing.

Jude had resisted the impulse to ring Sara Courtney until the Thursday, but with the synchronicity which had featured so much in her life, just as she was about to pick up the phone, Sara rang her.

'I've just seen the *Observer*,' she said, her voice high and taut, just as it had been when she first came to Jude.

'I thought you would. Or have heard about it on the news.'

'I haven't heard or seen any news till today. I've been away.'

'Well, if there's anything I can—'

'Jude, I need help. Can I come and see you?'

'Of course.'

'Jude, what I'm asking you to do is completely forget what I told you about seeing the body.' They were sitting in the cluttered sitting room of Woodside Cottage with cups of green tea.

'That may not be easy. The mind has a mind of its own. You can't just tell it to forget something.'

'Well, all right. Not forget it, but swear to me you'll never tell anyone about what I told you.'

Jude felt a little awkward, because she had already told someone – or that someone had winkled out of her – the details of what Sara had confided in her. But she said, 'I won't tell anyone', hoping that the implication was that she wouldn't tell anyone in the future. 'But what are *you* going to do, Sara?'

'How do you mean?'

'Well, the situation's changed rather. When you first told me about the body in the store room, you weren't even sure that you'd seen it. You were afraid you were hallucinating.'

'I'm still not sure I saw it.'

'Oh, come on. You can't claim that any more. The fact that you're here, the fact that you recognized the photo in the *Observer* – that must mean you *did* see Amos Green's body.'

Sara looked very crestfallen, but had to accept the truth of Jude's words.

'And was he someone you recognized?'

'Well, if I did see the body in the store room—'

'No, I mean did you recognize him in the photograph as someone you had met before – while he was still alive?'

Sara Courtney shook her head firmly. 'I'd never seen him before. And I wish I'd never seen him at all!'

'I can understand that.'

'I just want to forget that I ever saw him at all. Just wind back time.'

'Can't be done, I'm afraid. And the big change is that now the man's death is the subject of an official murder inquiry.'

'It wasn't necessarily murder. It could have been suicide.'

'Oh yes? And whereabouts did you tell me you'd seen the gun in the store room?'

'On the windowsill,' Sara had to admit.

'So, for the suicide theory to hold water, Amos Green must have shot himself in the temple, then, before falling down dead, have moved across the room to put the gun on the windowsill. Do you really believe that's what happened?'

'No,' came the grudging reply. 'But it's possible that he shot himself and the gun dropped to the floor as he fell down, and then someone else came in, found the body and moved the gun to the windowsill.'

'All right, I suppose it's possible. But who might have done that, Sara? Another member of Polly's Cake Shop staff? And, if they did do it, why didn't they tell anyone? Why didn't they raise the alarm? Why didn't they call the police?'

'They may have had their reasons. Like I did. I didn't call the police.'

'No, you didn't. But don't you think you should get in touch with them now?

'Why?' Sara Courtney sounded really frightened of the idea.

'Because you have evidence that is material to the police investigation. I don't know how much they know about Amos Green's movements before he died, but if he could be placed in Polly's Cake Shop's store room on the Saturday afternoon four weeks ago . . . well, I would imagine that would be of considerable help to their inquiries. What is more, presumably you still have the handkerchief with his blood on it. Now the police have a body, they could check the DNA on that.'

'Jude, you're not being very sympathetic.'

It was true. Jude realized she was behaving more like Carole might have done in the same circumstances. She was a healer. Her primary concern should be for her client rather than for some obscure ideal of justice.

'I'm sorry,' she said. 'I was just thinking you might feel better if you were to go to the police. Then you could put the whole business behind you.'

'I doubt that. It'd just get me more involved. I'm sure there'd be endless questioning. And I'd probably become a suspect for having murdered the poor bastard.'

'You'd soon be able to prove you had nothing to do with it.'

'Maybe. But I just don't feel strong enough for the stress of it all. Even though things seem finally to be going better for me, I'm still very fragile.'

'I know. But I'd be here to support you.'

'Yes, Jude. You'd be here. But you wouldn't be in the interview room when the police started grilling me about my entire life history, would you?'

Jude was forced to admit that was true. There was a silence. Then she asked, 'What did you mean by "things finally going better for you"?'

Sara blushed. 'Oh, nothing really. Just, you know, thanks to you and thanks to other factors, I do feel I'm finally emerging from the state I've been in since . . . well, since things went wrong. I feel continuing life is now a possibility.'

'And might one of the "other factors" be Kent Warboys?'

The blush deepened. 'I have seen him a few times. But we're taking things slowly. We're being discreet.'

Jude wondered how being seen by Ted Crisp 'all over each other' in the Crown & Anchor came under the heading of 'discreet', but all she said was, 'And it's going well?'

'I was beginning to dare to think so . . . but now I feel everything's been shattered again.' She looked pleadingly at Jude. 'I'm just terrified of going back down to where I was.'

'You won't go back there,' came the reassuring reply. 'Yes, you'll have setbacks, and each time you'll fear the whole cycle is starting again, but it won't. You'll bounce back more quickly every time it happens.'

Sara Courtney grunted dissent, not willing to believe this was true.

'Tell me about Kent. How did you meet him?'

'At Polly's. He came in a few times for coffee. He kept asking me questions. At first I thought he might be interested in me, but then I realized he was assessing the place, working out its development potential.'

'Was this after Quintus Braithwaite had asked him to become involved in the project?'

'Oh no, way before then. Kent had had his eyes on the development potential of Polly's and other properties on Fethering Parade for ages. The way he told it, he heard Quintus going on about the SPCS Action Committee in the yacht club and thought they might have mutual interests.'

Which wasn't exactly the way the Commodore had presented their connection, thought Jude without surprise.

'And, Sara, when you discovered that it was the property Kent was interested in, were you disappointed?'

Sara nodded. 'Yes. I felt stupid for having dared to hope that a man might even notice me. I went right back down to my lowest again. No confidence . . . thoughts of self-harming . . . you know, you've heard it all before.'

'Yes. But Kent came back?'

'Yes.'

'And no longer asking questions about development potential?'

'No. He asked me out for a drink. I thought he just wanted to pick my brains about Polly's, but he didn't mention the place. It was me he wanted to see.' She sounded bewildered by the idea.

'And why shouldn't he? You're gorgeous, Sara.'

'Huh. Anyway, we got together and then it seemed to cool off, and I got all paranoid again. But he got back in touch and the last few weeks . . . We even went away together for a couple of nights earlier in the week . . . Actually to Paris.'

'Very nice too.'

'Yes, it was. And I felt really good. And now I've come back to this. The photo on the front of the *Fethering Observer*. And I just don't need any more complications in my life.'

'I can see that. So you're not going to go to the police?'

'No,' said Sara Courtney firmly.

'Seeing the photo should have cheered you up, you know.'

'How do you work that out, Jude?'

'Because, at the most basic level, it proves you're not mad. When you saw the body, when you came to tell me about it, you didn't know whether you'd seen it or not. You thought you might be hallucinating. At least what you saw in the paper this morning proves that what you saw was real.'

'Yes. At the moment, though, I'm not sure whether that does make things better.'

'Of course it does,' said Jude briskly. Though the most empathetic person on God's earth, she knew there were times when people needed a little nudging along. 'So listen, Sara, you are faced with a dilemma. And I can't tell you what you should do about it. It's entirely your decision. Either you contact the police about what you saw in the store room at Polly's, or you don't. Over to you.'

Sara Courtney grimaced. 'I can't face it.'

'All right,' said Jude, being very careful to keep her voice unjudge-mental. 'Then what you saw in the store room at Polly's is a secret between the two of us.'

She felt bad about lying. But she didn't feel bad about having told Carole. Then something she saw in Sara's face made her ask, 'What, is there someone else who knows?'

The woman nodded. 'I did mention it to Kent.'

FOURTEEN

Having already compromised her principle of client confidentiality, Jude could see no reason to keep from Carole what she had just heard from Sara. The woman had not, after all, been talking in the context of a healing session.

Carole, predictably given her Home Office background, had disapproved of Sara's decision not to go to the police. 'It's the duty of every citizen to reveal any information they have that might be relevant to a police inquiry.'

'So you've always done that, have you, Carole?' asked Jude mischievously.

Her neighbour moved quickly on. There had been occasions during their previous investigations when Carole might have been accused of the same shortcoming as Sara. 'So, including Kent, there are now four people who know about what Sara saw in the store room.'

'Four we know of. There could be any number more. The police may be fighting off hundreds of witness statements from other people who saw the body. As is their custom, they're keeping the progress of their inquiries irritatingly quiet.'

'Yes.' Carole looked thoughtful. It was the Friday morning. They were in the spotless kitchen of High Tor. Gulliver snuffled by the Aga in another pleasant dream of chasing something. 'What we really need to find out is whether there is any connection between the deceased, Amos Green, and anyone else in Fethering.'

'What kind of connection?'

'That we don't know. Maybe there is no connection. Maybe his murderer just chose to dump the body – at least temporarily – in the store room of Polly's Cake Shop for reasons of his own. But I think the starting point of our investigation has to be looking for the connection.'

'So how *do* we start?'

'We start at the scene of the crime – or, if not that, the scene of the first discovery of the body.'

'Polly's Cake Shop?'

'Precisely. Someone there might know something.'

'Well, good luck trying to get anything out of Josie Achter. She is not the most sympathetic of interviewees. And she said she would never see me again.'

'She might see me.'

'I suppose everything's possible, but I'd be surprised if she did.'

'Worth asking.'

'Maybe. And under what pretext would you be wanting to see her?'

'As one of the people who found the body on Fethering Beach.'

'She will deny having any connection with the body on Fethering Beach. In fact, I'm pretty sure she does have no connection with the body on Fethering Beach.'

'I'll think of something, Jude.'

'Well, good luck.'

The number of the flat over Polly's was in the phone book, so Carole rang it as soon as Jude had gone back to Woodside Cottage to deal with a client.

The phone was answered by a young female voice. 'Hello?'

'Oh, good morning. My name is Carole Seddon. Is that Josie Achter?'

'No, it's her daughter Rosalie.'

'Is your mother there?'

'No, she's moved to a rented flat in Hove . . . just till the purchase of her own flat there goes through.'

'Ah, do you have a number for her there?'

'No.'

'A mobile?'

'No. My mother doesn't give out her mobile number.' Carole was meeting the level of co-operation Jude had warned her to expect.

'Could I leave a message for her?'

'What's it about?' the girl asked suspiciously.

'Well, I'm one of the people who found the man's body on Fethering Beach Thursday before last.'

'Oh, are you?' The tone of voice had changed to a mixture of caution and curiosity.

'Yes.'

'And why did you want to talk to my mother about that?'

'I'm talking to lots of people,' Carole lied. 'Trying to find out whether the dead man had any connection with Fethering.'

'Ah.' There was a silence. Then the girl said, 'I don't mind talking to you.'

Because it was lunchtime, Carole had intended only to have a small glass of Sauvignon Blanc, but Ted had already poured a large one before she could give her order. Rosalie asked for a vodka and tonic.

They sat opposite each other in one of the Crown and Anchor's alcoves. The pub's doors facing the sea, open all summer, had now been closed against the busy wind roaring up Fethering Beach. It was only just after twelve and they had the place more or less to themselves.

'Well, thank you for agreeing to talk to me,' said Carole once they'd clinked glasses.

'Not a problem.'

Like her mother, Rosalie Achter was one of the many people Carole knew by sight. She also knew their names, their employment and family circumstances, but she'd never actually spoken to them. She suspected that Rosalie Achter probably knew roughly the same amount about her. It was how things worked in Fethering.

'I wondered,' Rosalie went on, 'why you thought my mother might have anything to do with the body you discovered.'

'No particular reason. As I said, I'm talking to a lot of people.'

'Why?'

It was a good question, and one to which Carole had to scrabble around to find a good answer. To her annoyance, the only one she could come up with was rather flimsy and feminine. 'Well, I think it must be that actually finding that body was rather a shock. It's upset me more than I expected it to. I mean, it's not like I haven't seen a dead body before. But this one was in rather a horrible state and, I don't know, I just thought maybe finding out more about who he was might sort of humanize him, make him not so much a spook as a human being.'

The words didn't convince their speaker, but Rosalie Achter appeared not to hear anything odd in them. 'Well, presumably you've heard the news and seen the local paper?'

'Yes.'

'So you do actually know who he was?'

'Someone called Amos Green, yes.'

'And what makes you think he might have had something to do with my mother?'

The girl looked at her earnestly. Her hair was a brown so dark as to be nearly black. Though neatly shaped, it sprang out of her head in wiry profusion. Her features were sharp, eyes very black and skin dark. There was an almost manic quality to her body language and the way she spoke.

'As I say,' said Carole reassuringly, 'I'm just talking to people.'

Another limp answer, but fortunately Rosalie didn't seem to notice. 'Well, I'd never seen him before. I suppose it's possible my mother knew him before I was born, but I've never heard her mention anyone called Amos Green.'

'Have you spoken to her since he was formally identified?'

'Yes. She rang me yesterday.'

'And did she make any comment about the body?'

'She just repeated some of the things she's said before about Fethering.'

'Not enthusiastic?' asked Carole, remembering the report Jude had given of her encounter with Josie Achter.

'She loathes the place. She said that the finding of dead bodies on the beach could not make her hate Fethering more than she already does.'

'Quite extreme views.'

'My mother is a creature of extremes . . . as I have learned, spending the last eleven years living alone with her.'

'So you mean it's eleven years since your parents divorced?'

'Yes. Nearly twelve. Getting away to university was quite a relief, let me tell you. Even if I only went as far as Brighton. Getting away from all that Jewish crap my mother force-fed me with. I don't believe a word of it – don't think I ever did – but my mother kept on and on about it. At uni, though, I started for the first time in my life to be my own person. And there was no way I was going to live back here after I graduated.'

'So where are you living?'

'Still in Brighton. Got a very manky flat there, not in what the good people of Fethering would regard as a *nice area*, but at least it's my own.'

'You've bought it?'

'I wish. No, it's rented. When I say it's "my own", I mean that it's my own space, a space on which my mother can't encroach.'

'Ah. Brighton of course is not that far from Hove, where your mother is going to be in her new—'

'It's quite far enough away, thank you. And I've got a network of friends there – people my mother and the *nice people* of Hove wouldn't want to mix with. Given a bit of luck, I'll never have to see her again.'

'Ah. Local Fethering gossip used to say—'

'Carole, I've already stopped listening. I stop listening every time someone mentions "local Fethering gossip". It almost always means uninformed lies.'

'You may have a point. Anyway, one of the "uninformed lies" which had been going round Fethering was that you were going to take over the running of Polly's Cake Shop when your mother retired.'

'She may have had that idea. I never did.'

'But you studied Hospitality and Catering.'

'You can do that without going into a family business.'

'I agree. But you do still work for your mother at Polly's.'

'That's only because I haven't yet got my head together to do something else. When the sale of the place finally goes through, I'm off out of here.'

'You'll get a job in Brighton?'

'Probably. There's always plenty of bar work and waitressing around there.'

'Yes, I'm sure there is. Going back to your parents' divorce . . .'

'What about it?'

Carole, still recollecting the pains of her own split from David, trod carefully. 'Presumably that was a big trauma for you?'

'Yes. I was like twelve. It's not a great age to have your whole life suddenly turned upside down.'

'Do you still see your father?'

'Not very often. Not as often as I'd like to see him. If my mother had her way, I'd never see him.'

'Do you know what led to the divorce?'

'Meaning what?'

'Had either of them got someone else?'

'Not so far as I know. Though I wish for my father's sake that he had found someone. He deserved something nice in his life. I'm glad to say he has actually remarried since.'

'Were you at the wedding?'

'God, no. Not invited.' And the omission was clearly still a painful one.

'And as for your mother? Did she have someone else?'

'I wouldn't wish her on any man. All I recollect from the time they were together was my mother constantly sniping away at my father, criticizing him, undermining him. And she continued to do that right through my teens, all the time we were living in the flat over Polly's, just the two of us.' The girl's dark eyes glazed over. Carole was beginning to wonder whether the vodka and tonic was her first of the morning. 'I'd like to have had a relationship with my father. My mother saw to it that that was not possible.'

'And what about your own relationships?'

'How do you mean?'

'Did your mother encourage you to have boyfriends?'

'Hardly. I wouldn't have wanted to introduce any boy I fancied to her. Put him off me for life. So any relationships I did have I made sure she knew nothing about them. Which was fine once I got to uni.'

'And is fine now?'

'Are you asking me if I've got a boyfriend at the moment?'

'Well . . .'

'Bloody nosey, aren't you?' It was an accusation Carole would have been hard put to it to deny. 'Well, if you want to know, I had a long-term relationship which broke up four months ago. Since then it's been nothing but the odd one-night stand.'

'Are you still upset about it?'

'Still upset? I've been upset all my bloody life, as far back as I can remember. Anyone born to a mother like mine would be perma- nently upset.'

Carole rather wished she had Jude with her. The conversation was getting uncomfortably psychological, and Jude was always better at dealing with that stuff than she was.

'Going back to the body, the one I and my friend found on—'

'I know which body you're talking about. Incidentally, at the police press conference they said he'd been killed by a gunshot wound. Did you know that before you heard it from them?'

'Yes. My friend and I saw the bullet hole in his temple.'

'Ah. Anything else unusual you noticed?'

'Well, his legs appeared to have been tied together with rope, but that had broken.'

'And what did that make you think?'

'It made me think that perhaps the body had been tied to some heavy weight to take him down to the bottom of the sea. And when the rope broke he had floated free again.'

'Hm.' Rosalie Achter nodded her head thoughtfully. 'Did you suggest that to the police?'

'Sorry?'

'When the police interviewed you, did you mention your theory about him having been tied to a heavy weight?'

'No, I didn't. I've learnt over the years that the police don't take kindly to theories from unqualified amateurs. If the body had been weighted down, I'm sure they could have worked that out for themselves.'

'Yes.' The girl seemed obscurely pleased by the answer.

'When she first heard we'd found the body, did your mother pass any comment about it?'

'Like what?'

'Anything, really.'

'No. Well, I think she said, "Another bastard drowned after having a skinful – serves him right!" Something like that.'

'And when you spoke to her yesterday . . . you know, once the body had been identified as that of Amos Green . . . did she say anything about him then?'

'No. Why should she say anything about a person she'd never met before?'

Carole had to admit that she didn't know, really.

They seemed to have finished their conversation about the same time they'd finished their drinks. Neither suggested a refill. Rosalie said she had to get back to Polly's for her 'bloody shift'.

Carole was thoughtful as she walked back to High Tor. What interested her most was not the girl's belligerence towards her mother but, given the negative reactions Rosalie had given to all Carole's questions, why she had so readily agreed to meet in the first place.

FIFTEEN

Jude was surprised by a knock on her front door on the following morning, the Saturday. She opened it to reveal a woman in her sixties wearing a pale blue linen dress. Her grey hair was cut in a stylish pageboy bob and she wore large dark-rimmed glasses.

'Good morning,' she said. 'My name is Janice Green and I believe you are one of the people who found my husband's body on Fethering Beach last week.'

Jude had called through to Carole and now the three women were sitting over coffee on the draped armchairs of Woodside Cottage's sitting room. Carole and Jude made appropriate comments of condolence, but Janice Green swept them aside.

'What I'm currently feeling about Amos's death is more surprise than intense bereavement. I fell out of love with him many years ago.' Her words were not bitter or self-pitying, more matter-of-fact.

'But,' she went on, 'I am obviously intrigued as to how he died. I've been questioned by the police who seem convinced he committed suicide but, needless to say, they aren't vouchsafing me much information. So, having read in the paper about you two having found his body, I thought I'd come and see if you had any useful information.'

'Which paper was it you saw the news in?' asked Carole. 'The *Fethering Observer*?'

'No. *Daily Mail*. His death did make the national news. That would have pleased Amos, I think. Fame at last.' She read in their faces that some explanation was required. 'My husband didn't lack self-esteem.'

'And how did you find out where we lived?' asked Carole.

'Oh, I thought Fethering was the kind of place where everyone would know everyone – particularly if they had the notoriety of having found a body on the beach, so I asked in a café near the front.'

'Polly's Cake Shop?'

'Yes.'

Carole and Jude exchanged looks. It was probably just coincidence that Janice Green had entered the premises where her husband's body had been found before its immersion in the sea. But on the other hand . . .

'I read in the paper,' said Jude, 'that your husband lived in Kingston.'

'Yes, he did.'

'You imply that that was in the past.'

'We hadn't cohabited for over five years. Amos moved out.'

'And where had he been living since?'

The strangely unemotional widow shrugged. 'He shacked up with some woman. Whether he was still with the same one when he died I don't know. I would have thought it was unlikely. His flings didn't tend to last very long. He could have shacked up with a good few since I last saw him.'

'Do you have children?' asked Jude.

'No. Possibly one of the many reasons why our relationship didn't work out.' She was still brusquely unsentimental. 'Anyway, would you mind telling me about when you found his body?'

'There's not a lot to tell,' said Carole.

'Never mind. Any detail you can remember. I thought I had firmly closed the book on the chapter of my life that involved Amos, but since I heard of his death, it seems to have opened itself up again.'

So Carole and Jude told her exactly what they had seen. At first, out of sensitivity, they did not describe the state of the corpse as they had found it. But Janice wanted every last detail. And remained unflinching as they supplied them.

At the end of their narrative, she said, 'Thank you. I wonder whose husband he'd pissed off this time.'

Carole looked at her curiously. 'Are you suggesting that he might have been killed by a jealous husband?'

'Of course that's what I'm saying. Amos had antagonized a good few in his time. More than one of them had come after him. A couple even beat him up. So I assume there was one who took rather more extreme measures.'

'You don't buy the police's suicide theory?'

She shook her head firmly. 'No. And surely the ropes that were found round his ankles would knock that on the head. They must have been fixed to something to weigh the body down.'

'That was the conclusion we had come to,' said Carole.

'Apart from anything else, nobody who knew Amos would ever believe that he'd kill himself. As I said, far too much self-esteem. Amos thought he was God's gift . . . not just to women but to the entire world.' For the first time a note of exasperated affection came into her voice. 'And he did have a lot of charm. Most people were bowled over when they first met him. I certainly was. He was a difficult man to dislike.'

'Unless you were the husband of one of the women he went after?' Jude suggested.

'Yes.' A grin. 'Or unless you were married to him. As I say, a charmer. Had that wonderful self-deprecating Jewish humour. Always bouncing upright again after every setback, like one of those Wobbly men. Great to be with, great to have a fling with, very poor husband material.'

'Did you tell the police,' asked Jude, 'that you didn't believe he'd committed suicide?'

'Oh yes. And they clearly thought it was just another distraught widow unable to come to terms with the fact that her husband had felt miserable enough to do such a thing. Which was not the case at all. As you see, I'm far from distraught. Just curious.'

'Mm,' said Carole, still a little surprised by the woman's lack of emotion. 'You've talked about your husband's private life. What about work? Was he successful there? The paper said he was a chartered surveyor.'

'Yes, he scraped through the exams and then proceeded to do as little work as possible for the rest of his career. He travelled a lot, working on different projects round the country, and became a past master at fiddling his expenses.' She checked herself. 'I may be being slightly unfair there. I think when he first qualified he did have some principles – aspirations, even. I hadn't met him then, but from things he said I think he did have some ideals about ecology, sustainable development, that kind of stuff. But it didn't last. Contact with the real world of wheeler-dealing and back-scratching soon made him cynical and selfish.'

Jude came in, 'The paper also said he used to be a local councillor. Surely you have to have some sense of public duty to do that?'

'Maybe Amos started out with that too. He became a councillor very young. By the time I met him, he'd given it up and was only out for what he could get.'

'Were you his first wife?' asked Carole.

'Yes. And in retrospect I don't for the life of me know why he wanted to get married. He seemed to be having a very good time flitting from flower to flower – and the amount of travelling he did made that all the easier. Maybe he thought marriage would settle him down. Well, if that was his plan, it didn't work.' Again there was no self-pity in her voice. 'Anyway, it soon became clear to me that he wasn't going to let the existence of a marriage licence curtail his extramarital activities.'

'How long ago were you married?' asked Jude.

'Twenty-three years. Amazing we lasted that long, isn't it? As I said, it soon became clear that Amos was going to be a serial adulterer. And I was faced with the choice of putting up or shutting up. Maybe if I'd found someone else, I might have felt the need to get divorced. But that didn't happen, so we continued to cohabit.'

'Until four years ago?'

'Yes.'

'Was there a particular reason why he walked out?'

'Like what?'

'Like,' suggested Jude, 'Amos meeting someone new; someone he really fell for?'

Janice shrugged. 'Possibly. He did retain a romantic streak. He still embarked on each new relationship as if it was going to be the big thing, the real thing. But after a few weeks he always started looking elsewhere.'

'Did he have any children?' asked Carole. 'You know, out of wedlock?'

'Not so far as I know.'

'And over the years, with his multiple infidelities, were you aware of any that really got through to him, that hurt him, perhaps, when the woman broke it off?'

'It wasn't the kind of thing he confided in me, obviously. And I think he generally made a point of ending things himself before the woman had the opportunity to get tired of him. He was a very shrewd operator,' Janice concluded with grudging admiration.

'But was there any time when Amos seemed particularly on edge while you knew he was having an affair?'

'Not really.' Janice Green looked thoughtful. 'Well, there was a time, way back, just after we got married, when he did seem particularly tense. I'd forgotten about it till you asked, but yes, he was in quite a state. A worse state than I've seen him in since. In retrospect I think he was probably just tense because it was the first time he'd been unfaithful since we'd got married, and he was waiting to see how I'd react. And I was terribly upset at the time, so my recollection may not be completely accurate. But after that I kind of reconciled myself – not enthusiastically but effectively – to the kind of man I had married and let him go his own sweet way. And once Amos realized that he'd got away with it once, he didn't get so uptight about his subsequent dalliances.'

'And do you know who the woman was, that first time?' asked Carole.

'No idea. I fairly quickly came to the conclusion that the only way I was going to cope with an adulterous husband was by shutting my mind to all the details of his affairs.'

Jude nodded and said, 'I understand that.' Prompting immediate suspicion from Carole that her neighbour had once experienced a similar situation. Jude's love life was much more extensive and varied in Carole's imagination than it ever was in reality.

'Anyway . . .' Janice Green reached for her handbag. 'I've taken up quite enough of your time. Thank you for talking to me.'

'I hope it's helped,' said Jude.

'I think it has, in a way. I think it will help me finally to close that chapter I talked about.'

'Good luck.'

'Thank you.'

'And if we get any more information, you know, about what happened to your husband . . . would you like us to keep you informed?'

Janice Green sighed wearily. 'Do you know, I don't think I'm that bothered. I talked about "closing a chapter", and somehow I think coming here this morning has helped me do that. It's reinforced the feeling that I never did really know anything about Amos. And I think for the time being, I'll leave things like that. I'm not keen to open the chapter again.'

'So if we do find out anything else . . .?'

'Why not tell the police? That's the right thing to do, isn't it? Then if they think what you've told them has any relevance to my life, well, they can get in touch with me, can't they?' Janice Green stood up.

'Just one more question before you go,' said Carole.

'Mm?'

'Apart from a jealous husband, can you think of anyone else who might have wanted to kill your husband?'

'No. As I said, it was difficult not to like Amos. Most people did . . . except for jealous husbands.'

As Jude saw Janice Green out of the front door, she reflected on the different ways in which different people coped with bereavement.

SIXTEEN

There was no news of an inquest on Amos Green. No news at all about Amos Green, as October slipped into November. Carole became prematurely obsessed with what she was going to give her two granddaughters for Christmas.

Jude continued a busy programme of healing. She didn't hear much from Sara Courtney, which was good news. Not because she didn't want to hear from her, but the fact that Sara was uncommunicative indicated that mentally she was healthy. And on the one occasion in November that Jude saw her in Polly's Cake Shop, she gathered that her mental health was in no small measure due to the development of her relationship with Kent Warboys. All of which was excellent news.

Carole and Jude were frustrated by their lack of progress on the investigation of Amos Green's murder, but there didn't seem much they could do. Though they spoke on the phone to the dead man's widow, she could add little to what she had told them at Woodside Cottage. She was, however, annoyed that the police had not yet released her late husband's body, and so she couldn't arrange the funeral which she hoped would bring final closure to that chapter of her life.

Carole and Jude seemed to have no further leads to follow. And, as ever, they had no idea what was going on in the official inquiry. Carole was of the opinion that the police were probably building up evidence to ensure that, when the inquest finally happened, the coroner would have no difficulty in passing a verdict of suicide.

Early in November there was another meeting of the SPCS Action Committee. And it was clear, in spite of Quintus Braithwaite's customary bluster, that the impetus for action was trickling away. Except for the announcement that the order for SPCS Action Committee headed notepaper had been put through to 'these very good people Phoebe knows in London', nothing much seemed to have advanced since the previous meeting.

Numbers attending were down. There were considerably more

'apologies' recorded under the first item on the Agenda. Jude herself had been tempted just not to turn up and effect her resignation by continuing non-appearance rather than by any public statement.

But some residual loyalty to Sara did drag her along to Hiawatha, where she was royally bored. Flora Claire went on at great length about her latest idea for an alternative use for Polly's Cake Shop, as a Naturopathic Health Centre as well as a café. She tried to inveigle Jude into this plan, saying that her brand of healing would be a fitting complement to the hot stone massage, body brushing and chocolate spa treatments that she was envisaging. Jude was uncharacteristically sharp in her rejection of any possible involvement. Her healing was a private and serious business, not a pampering resource for the idle rich of West Sussex.

When they got on to the Agenda item 'Publicity and Profile', Lesley Tarquin once again whipped out her iPad mini. On this occasion she was dressed in ultra-tight black leggings and a pink silk top so diaphanous that everyone knew she was wearing a red bra. Quintus Braithwaite's eyes burned with ill-concealed lust every time he looked at her.

Lesley assured the committee that she was still in close contact with Vince at the *Fethering Observer* and was in regular touch with the *West Sussex Gazette* and *Sussex Life*. Jezza from FOAM FM was still on board, as were Will at Radio Solent and Flick at Radios Surrey and Sussex. And it would only need a phone call for Barry at *South Today* and Fizz at Meridian to drop everything and rush to Fethering to cover the next SPCS Action Committee event.

Lesley was unfazed when Wendy Roote was uncharitable enough to ask whether she had actually got any publicity for anything yet. No, she said she was as yet just 'getting her ducks in a row', so that she could 'co-ordinate a big media splash' when 'the time was right'. Wendy persisted, asking when the time might be right, and Lesley replied that it would be when the SPCS Action Committee had a 'mega-story' with which they could 'carpet-bomb the punters'.

Quintus Braithwaite said that all sounded very good. Then he and Arnold Bloom became involved in a long argument on the choice of venue for the next meeting, which stayed only just the right side of insulting. (In fact Arnold Bloom's description of the interior décor of Hiawatha probably was insulting.)

After 'Any Other Business', when diaries were brought out to arrange 'Date of Next Meeting', the level of unavailability or uncertainty about availability amongst the committee members and the argument as to whether Wednesdays were the best night for meetings suggested that the SPCS Action Committee, like so many local initiatives before it, was about to spiral away into nothingness. Jude didn't think she would have to tender her formal resignation. Pretty soon there wouldn't be any committee for her to resign from.

She was therefore very surprised to receive the following day an email summoning her to an EGM of the SPCS Action Committee at Hiawatha on the following Monday. The reason was not explained. When Jude mentioned this to her neighbour, whose Home Office experience meant she knew her way around committee protocol, Carole said this was illegal. Members of a committee summoned to an Extraordinary General Meeting must be informed of the purpose of the meeting, otherwise any resolutions they pass are invalid.

Jude rationalized that the EGM had probably been called to accelerate the process whose symptoms she had witnessed at Wednesday night's meeting. The SPCS Action Committee was about to be put out of its misery and wound up.

She couldn't have been more wrong.

Though the coup that was announced on the Monday evening at Hiawatha was not Quintus Braithwaite's, characteristically he wanted to claim credit for it. So he took a long time to weave his introduction to the evening's undoubted star.

'. . . and I like to think that our efforts on the SPCS Action Committee have helped to raise the profile of Polly's Cake Shop and the issue of its survival and the form in which it survives. It is often the case – frequently through the input of organizations like this one which I have initiated – that ground-roots lobbying produces better results than approaches through more official channels. And I think that is undoubtedly the case in this instance.

'I am very pleased that my idea of bringing Kent Warboys into our discussions has proved so fruitful. Because Kent has some news for us.'

The Commodore smiled patronizingly at the younger man, as though introducing his protégé. Jude remembered what Sara had told her about Kent being interested in Polly's Cake Shop long before Quintus Braithwaite ever talked to him about it.

But the architect wasn't about to mention that fact. If the Chair of the SPCS Action Committee wanted to take on unmerited glory, that didn't bother him.

Instead, he grinned around at the group in Hiawatha's sitting room. (There was a much better turnout than there had been the previous Wednesday. The announcement of an 'EGM' prompted cheering hopes for some scandal or disaster.)

'The fact is,' said Kent Warboys, 'that you are currently looking at the owner of Polly's Cake Shop.'

The committee burst into spontaneous applause.

'My lawyers completed the necessary formalities on Friday. I paid the asking price for the premises, though some of my commercial estate-agent advisers thought it was rather steep.'

So Josie Achter had got her pound of flesh, thought Jude; then had a momentary anxiety that the reference might be thought anti-Semitic. She reassured herself that it wasn't, but reflected how cautious Josie's hypersensitivity on the subject had made her.

'But my concern,' Kent Warboys continued, 'has always been – even if it meant paying a bit over the odds – to secure the Polly's Cake Shop premises for the community of Fethering. And that has now been achieved.

'My plans for the development of the site – you know, for the affordable housing at the back – are still being finalized. Then they'll have to go through the local planning process—'

'Which can be a nightmare,' interrupted Arnold Bloom, who knew about such matters (and also thought that Quintus Braithwaite and Kent Warboys had so far monopolized the evening's proceedings to his disadvantage).

'Yes, I agree it can be.' Kent Warboys smiled knowingly. 'But I do like to think I have a good track record with them . . . after the work I've done on the Smalting Lifeboat Centre and the Clincham Haymarket Gallery.' Once again the names of these projects drew approving nods from the committee. If the Polly's Cake Shop development matched the standards of those two environment-friendly schemes, no one would have any worries.

'So I like to think I've built up a level of trust – even respect – with the local planning committees. They are aware of the architectural values that I hold dear. As I always say to them, "I'm a Warboy, not a Cowboy."' This was clearly a line he'd used on many occasions, but it still brought a friendly titter from the assembly. 'So I'm optimistic about the response we're likely to get from the planners. Though it'll all take time, of course, I'm aware of that, I am confident that the outcome will be positive.'

'But I think, Kent,' said Quintus Braithwaite, fearing he was losing his central position in the evening's proceedings, 'that you have something even more important to announce to the committee.'

'Yes, I was getting there.' The architect spoke without reproof. If he was riled by the Commodore's obsessive stage-managing of the evening, he didn't let it show.

'The main point is that since I am – or rather my company, Warboys Heritage Construction is – now the owner of Polly's, I can decide what happens to the place in the immediate future – you know, before we get into the business of planning and structural work.

'And what I would like to do is to move as quickly as possible to running Polly's Cake Shop as a Community Project just in the way that this committee envisages!'

This was the big announcement of the evening and it was greeted with warm and sustained applause.

'What you mean,' asked Wendy Roote, who liked to have everything in her life clearly defined, 'is that Josie Achter is no longer in charge of Polly's Cake Shop but we are?'

'That is exactly what I mean.'

'And does Josie know about that?'

'Yes. I've had a few meetings with her – and your Treasurer sat in on a couple of them.' Alec Walters inclined his head to confirm this. 'But Josie Achter seemed completely unconcerned about what happened to the café after she'd sold it.'

'So how would the day-to-day running of the place work?' Wendy persisted.

'What I'm proposing in the short term,' Kent Warboys replied, 'is that the café will continue to be run by the existing staff, for whom I will pick up the tab, paying them exactly what Josie Achter did, until we've sorted out how it's going to work with the community running it.'

'But how do we know,' said Arnold Bloom, 'that you won't find that running the place yourself is rather lucrative and you'll want to keep on being in charge?'

'I can assure you,' said Kent Warboys evenly, still showing no signs of annoyance, 'that amongst the many ambitions I have held at one time or another, running a café is not one of them. No, I'm just talking about the next few weeks, while you're sorting out how the community organization of the place is going to work.'

'Well, it'll be done by volunteers,' said Quintus Braithwaite, as though the answer was self-evident.

'Right, if that's the way it's going to be done, fine.'

'My wife Phoebe is highly skilled in organizing volunteers. While we were posted in Dar es Salaam, she established a wonderful organization to set up coffee mornings for the wives of local sailors. All done by volunteers.'

'Excellent. I'm sure there are many people in Fethering whose talents we can call on to ensure the smooth running of the project. But it is going to take a few weeks to get the whole thing up and running.'

'Not long, you know.' The Commodore chuckled. 'In the Navy we have a reputation for sorting things out quickly. We'll have the volunteers' rota set up in no time.'

'Well, let's see how that goes,' said Kent Warboys. 'You just keep me informed of your timescale. Fortunately we're entering a time of the year when business at Polly's slackens off, so we should be able to make the changes gradually.'

'I think what we need to do,' enthused Lesley Tarquin, 'is to have a major relaunch when the café's taken over by the community. That's the kind of project the local press loves – ticks all the right boxes about sustainability, historical continuity and Big Society enterprise. We could get just mega-coverage for an event like that.'

'Excellent idea,' said Quintus Braithwaite, who was still not very good at concealing his attraction towards the youngest and most glamorous member of his committee. She was looking very good that day in a shocking pink top and silver leggings. In spite of her greyed hair, she still contrived to make all the other women present look frumpy.

'I was thinking it might be good to have the launch just before Christmas,' said Lesley. 'I've done some market research with local traders and they say the Parade gets busy round then. Be a good time to stage a massive media blitz.'

'Good thinking,' said the Commodore. 'We'll discuss the fine-tuning at the next meeting.'

'Could I just ask one thing?' said Jude, 'Is the plan for Polly's, once it becomes a Community Project, to have the entire business run by volunteers?'

'Why shouldn't it be?' asked the Commodore.

'Well, I'd have thought there might be an argument for employing a paid manager to keep an eye on—'

'Nonsense! We won't need anyone like that.' Quintus Braithwaite was beginning to sound distinctly testy.

'Also,' asked Flora Claire, 'how soon should we start exploring the other uses we're going to put the café to? Can we do that straight away – you know, developing a Mindfulness Centre and—?'

'There will not be any bloody Mindfulness Centre!' came the even testier reply.

'And will Polly's have to close down for a while?' asked Wendy Roote. 'You know, for refurbishment?'

Kent Warboys fielded that one. 'I had thought of that possibility. And as a gesture of goodwill, and because I believe strongly in helping start-ups, my company is prepared to put up twenty grand for any basic refurbishment that's required, so that doesn't have to come out of the SPCS Action Committee budget.'

Through the applause that greeted this, Arnold Bloom was heard to ask whether the SPCS Action Committee actually had a budget. The Commodore assured him that it was all in the hands of their Treasurer. Alec Walters agreed that the budget was in his hands, but wished to point out that the SPCS Action Committee did not actually have any funds. Kent Warboys' offer of twenty grand was very generous, but maybe they should also think of other forms of fundraising.

Quintus Braithwaite then took it upon himself to give the Treasurer and everyone else present a lesson in economics. 'Fundraising may be necessary in time, though I doubt if it actually will. Now the major costs of running a small business like Polly's Cake Shop is always going to be paying the staff. There are obviously other expenses like maintenance of the building, purchase of the food and drink, but those are tiny next to the staffing. And of course, the way this place is going to be run from now on, we won't have any staffing costs!'

'How do you mean?' asked Wendy Roote.

'What I'm saying is that when Polly's is up and running as a Community Project, we won't have any paid staff. It will all be run by volunteers!'

'Do you mean,' asked Jude, thinking of Sara Courtney's job, 'that all the existing staff are going to be sacked?'

'That's a harsh way of putting it, Jude. The existing staff will be given notice and, if they wish to, they will work out their notice in accordance with the existing employment laws. And after they've left, any of them will of course be at liberty to come back as volunteers.'

'Unpaid?' asked Jude.

'That is normally what the word "volunteer" implies.'

Jude was tempted to launch into a diatribe about how such working arrangements might be fine for Phoebe and her circle of Joannas or Samanthas, whose husband's salaries and pensions could fund whatever daytime activities they chose to indulge in. But how the situation was rather different for people like Sara. And probably for people like Binnie the waitress and Hammo the cook.

But before she could manage to introduce some social politics into the proceedings, Flora Claire raised another issue. 'I think, like, it's really good that Kent has, like, made this offer of twenty grand. That's really cool, but I think we should, like, prioritize how that money's going to be spent. You know, like, can we agree to put, say, five grand of it aside to develop the Mindfulness Centre element of Polly's? And how are we going to fund the start-up of the Naturopathy bit of the—?'

'Listen!' Quintus Braithwaite roared. 'All of these questions can and will be dealt with at a separate committee meeting . . . where I am sure they will be treated with the seriousness that they deserve.' There was a distinctly sceptical sneer in the last few words. 'The sole purpose of tonight's EGM was for Kent to pass on to us the glad news that his company now owns Polly's Cake Shop. Which

is the first of what I'm sure will be many triumphs for the SPCS
Action Committee that I set up. The fine-tuning we will sort out at
a later date. The only decision we need to make tonight is about
the change of name for the café.'

'Why does it need a change of name?' asked Jude.

Arnold Bloom agreed. 'It's been Polly's Cake Shop on Fethering
Parade for years. It's a local landmark. We don't want to change
that.'

'I think we need to,' the Chair countered, 'to symbolize the new
direction the café will be taking.'

'We need no such thing. What the Fethering community always
wants is continuity. We find that with almost every issue that is
brought up at the Fethering Village Committee. To change the name
would be—'

'I think we should put this to the vote straight away,' said Quintus
Braithwaite, keen to take advantage of the supportive mood of the
committee. 'By a show of hands. If you agree that Polly's Cake
Shop should henceforth be known as Polly's Community Café, will
you please—?'

'You can't do that!' protested Arnold Bloom. 'That word "community" is the kiss of death to any commercial enterprise.' Jude was
surprised. He was the last person she would have expected to share
the views of Carole Seddon.

The Commodore continued unperturbed, 'So those in favour of the
change of name, please raise your right hand . . .'

He won the vote overwhelmingly, and derived great pleasure from
the expression of disgruntlement on Arnold Bloom's face.

'So what I wish to do now is to close this meeting and to . . .'
he raised his voice, shouting towards the kitchen '. . . *ask the lovely
Phoebe to bring in the champagne with which we are going to toast
Kent Warboys' good news!*'

The lovely Phoebe, who had been waiting for her cue behind the
kitchen door, came hurrying in to the sitting room with trays of champagne bottles and flutes to celebrate this wonderful breakthrough.

During the impromptu party that followed, Arnold Bloom was
heard to mutter that the SPCS Action Committee wasn't Quintus
Braithwaite's own bloody project, it was a Community bloody
Project for all the residents of Fethering. And he reiterated that,
though he was a great supporter of the principle of 'community',

the use of the word attached to any business project was the 'absolute kiss of death'.

Arnold was also heard to mutter that he wasn't 'the kind of man to be bought off by bribes of the Braithwaites' champagne'. That didn't stop him from drinking quite a lot of it, though.

SEVENTEEN

I t was two days later that Jude received a telephonic summons from Phoebe Braithwaite. Could she come at ten o'clock the following morning, the Thursday, for coffee at Hiawatha? Jude suggested it might be more convenient for them to meet at the Crown and Anchor or Polly's Cake Shop, but those venues did not fit in with Phoebe's preconceived plans. Maybe, like her husband, she liked to ensure home advantage.

Part of Jude wanted to tell Phoebe to get lost, but saying something like that was not in her nature. She was intrigued too as to what her conspiratorial hostess wanted to talk to her about. And a residual investigative instinct in connection with Amos Green's death made her want to glean any information she could about anyone with a connection to Polly's Cake Shop.

Jude felt her customary claustrophobia as she entered the Shorelands Estate. Though the main gates were never closed it did still have the feeling of a 'gated community'. The list of regulations behind glass on a board nearby also seemed designed to discourage freedom. Presumably the Shorelands residents knew when they were allowed to mow their lawns and hang out their washing, so having the list as the first thing visitors saw presumably had the sole aim of making them realize just how exclusive the estate was.

The whole complex with its huge, expensive, well-spaced houses in a variety of architectural styles felt about as welcoming to Jude as Colditz.

She hadn't known what to expect. Maybe this would be a large meeting with a lot of Joannas and Samanthas. But it was clear when she arrived and was ushered into the state-of-the-art kitchen that the occasion was just going to be a *tête-à-tête* for her and Phoebe Braithwaite.

While her hostess busied herself with the state-of-the-art Italian coffee machine, Jude looked out at the best view of the house. A long, over-titivated garden, all of whose plants had been dragooned into straight lines, sloped down towards a tall fence with double gates in it. Beyond that, because of the gradient, the mess of dunes, shingle and khaki sand could not be seen. Just the sparkling of the English Channel, which turned bluer the further it was away from the shore.

Against the fence at the end of the garden stood a neat hut and a blue rowing boat on a manoeuvrable two-wheeled trailer. Along the top of the fence and gates were coils of razor wire. Undesirable people would at all costs be kept out of the Shorelands Estate.

'Anyway,' said Phoebe as she placed their coffees on the table (showing off the range of her Italian machine, she was having a skinny latte, Jude a cappuccino with sugar), 'the first thing you must do is have a look at this.' She gestured to an expensive-looking blue cardboard box on the table in front of Jude.

'May I open it?'

'Of course.'

The contents were revealed to be very good-quality headed note-paper. Under a naval-looking design involving an anchor and a cannon was the legend: 'SPCS Action Committee'. Centred beneath that in the same large font were the words: 'Chair: Commodore Quintus Braithwaite'. No other names featured.

Jude did rather tentatively recall that there had been an agreement that the committee's other officers should get a name-check, but Phoebe swiftly swept away that objection, saying, 'No, it's a design thing. The little girl from the printers who advised us on layout – charming she is, ex-Roedean – said it'd look bolder with just the one name.'

Bolder maybe, thought Jude, but not what the committee voted for. However, she kept her opinion to herself.

Phoebe smiled at her ferociously. 'Now, I'm sure you'd like to know the reason why I wanted to have this little chat.'

'Well, I was mildly intrigued, yes.' Jude was once again struck by how confident Phoebe Braithwaite was in the absence of her husband. Gone was the twitchy nervousness that she'd demonstrated when lurking in the kitchen during committee meetings. Now she was a woman fully in control of everything – to the point of actu-ally being bossy. Jude wondered whether the twittery Phoebe was an act created during the course of their marriage to build up her husband's confidence and demonstrate her utter dependence on him.

It wouldn't be the first time she had seen the same kind of ritual in a relationship.

'Well, it was, needless to say, in connection with Polly's Cake Shop that I wanted to talk to you, what with you being on the committee and everything . . .'

Jude thought she should sound an early note of caution. 'I may not be staying on the committee for very long.'

'No, but you are on it at the moment, which means that you must be in favour of Quintus's plans for the development of Polly's Cake Shop as a Community Project.'

The logic of what Phoebe had just said would not have stood up to close scrutiny, but Jude let it pass as her hostess went on, 'Now would you believe that muggins here has got delegated to sort out the Volunteer Rota for when the Community Project starts.'

And I wonder who did the delegating, thought Jude, and had no difficulty finding an answer. It struck her that Quintus Braithwaite had no right to take that kind of decision off his own bat. The organizer of the Volunteer Rota was an appointment that should be made by the whole SPCS Action Committee. Though Jude herself didn't care about the niceties of 'meeting protocol', she knew a lot of her colleagues on the committee would deeply resent the Commodore's unilateral action. But she got the feeling the Braithwaites were very practised in running things their own way.

She was also amused by Phoebe's reference to 'muggins here', implying that she had unwillingly taken on the burden of the Volunteer Rota rather than being chuffed to bits at being given the responsibility.

'Now, a little bird told me, Jude, that in the course of your varied career, you did at one stage work in a restaurant . . .' It was true, but how did she know that? Jude didn't let the question trouble her for long. She had lived in Fethering long enough never to be surprised by the efficiency of its bush telegraph. Any piece of information dropped casually into conversation with anyone very quickly became public property. Fethering had had its own highly efficient non-electronic social media long before the creation of Facebook or Twitter.

'So I was wondering,' Phoebe went on, 'whether when we set up Polly's as a Community Project, we could count on your expertise . . .?'

'In what way?' came the cautious reply.

'Well, you know, pick your brains about things.'

'My brains are open for picking at any time. You're welcome to anything you can find in them.'

'Thank you, that's very generous.' Phoebe Braithwaite smiled graciously. 'The fact is, I also wondered whether you might be ready to help in a more active capacity . . .?'

The 'Oh?' with which Jude responded was also cautious.

'I think we're so fortunate in Fethering to have such a wonderful supply of hidden talents. You meet people for the first time and you know nothing of their history, and then slowly you discover that there are all these things they can do. I mean, for instance, until Quintus mentioned it on Monday, a lot of people didn't know about my running coffee mornings when we were posted to Dar es Salaam. And I mean, I'm not blowing my own trumpet about it or saying that I did anything particularly wonderful out there, but the fact remains that the whole thing was my initiative and, though I say it myself, it was damn well run.'

'I'm not quite sure how this relates to my experience in restaurants.'

'No, well, it was just an example about hidden talents. And I was thinking that, with you having worked in a restaurant . . . I mean, what exactly did you do?'

'It was a long time ago, but I suppose I . . . well, I helped out with the cooking when required, but basically I ran the place.'

'You were, kind of, the manager?'

'Yes.'

Jude wondered whether Phoebe had picked up on what she'd said on Monday about Polly's Cake Shop possibly needing a paid manager, and was planning the excuses that she would make if offered the job, when Phoebe said, 'Well, I was wondering whether I could include you in my rota of volunteer waitresses?'

Jude was too shocked to speak. The way the offer was put forward, it was as though she were being offered a rich gift, of which she was not really worthy.

'I mean, obviously,' Phoebe Braithwaite went on, 'I do have to have a quality control of the people who act as waitresses for Polly's. We have standards to maintain. And some of my friends were a little dubious as to whether I should ask you.'

I see, thought Jude, with a seething fury that rarely visited her. My name has been bandied round with all the Joannas or Samanthas to see if I qualify to be one of their number.

But Phoebe hadn't finished. 'Some of them thought you dressed a bit scruffily, you know, and ought to spruce up appearance-wise.' She smiled magnanimously. 'But I came to your rescue and pointed out to them that, as a waitress, you would be wearing the black and white livery of Polly's Cake Shop – or whatever livery we end up using – so nobody would see what you normally wore. And then some of them said: What about your hair? But I assured them that it was not beyond the wit of man to come up with a less flamboyant style which would fit neatly under a Polly's mobcap. So I was very much your defender, Jude, and I said you should definitely be considered as one of our volunteer waitresses,' she concluded, Lady Bountiful graciously vouchsafing charity to her inferior.

'Well, thank you very much,' said Jude with an uncharacteristic iciness. 'I am obviously very grateful for your offer. But what you seem to be forgetting is that I already have a full-time job.'

'Do you?' Phoebe Braithwaite looked confused for a moment, but then reminded herself, 'Of course, you do that healing business, don't you? But surely that's only a side-line?'

'It is my profession,' said Jude with some dignity, 'and it is one whose demands, I'm afraid, preclude the possibility of my taking on any other work, voluntary or otherwise.'

'Oh well, that's that then,' said Phoebe, not sounding too upset by the reaction. 'Just as well, probably. There were still one or two of the others who were a bit dubious about including you.'

Jude, who was not very good about staying angry for long, found that her mood was shifting. The humour of the situation now seemed more compelling than its offensiveness. That Phoebe Braithwaite could be completely unaware of how insulting she was being . . . Jude couldn't wait to tell Carole about it.

Another thought struck her at the same time. The public announce-ment of Kent Warboys' purchase of Polly's Cake Shop had been made at the EGM on the Monday. Only three days before. Phoebe Braithwaite hadn't had time to marshal all her Joannas or Samanthas into a Volunteer Rota by then. Quintus must have tipped her the wink and she must have started her planning before the news was public knowledge. That casual disregard for democracy, she was beginning to realize, would have been entirely characteristic behaviour for the Braithwaites.

'Anyway, Phoebe,' she said, 'I'm sure you'll be able to find a full rota of volunteer waitresses without me.'

'Yes,' Phoebe agreed, 'no problem about that.'

Now, as each unwitting insult slammed home, Jude was beginning to feel an irresistible instinct to giggle. To avoid giving into it, she looked out down Hiawatha's back garden towards the sea. 'Lovely position you have here,' she said, just as if she were one of Phoebe Braithwaite's regular coterie of Joannas or Samanthas.

'Oh, it is, isn't it?'

'Pity you have to have the razor wire on the fence and gates.'

'Oh, I couldn't agree with you more, Jude. So unsightly, isn't it? But I'm afraid one has to adjust to the times one lives in, doesn't one? I'd get rid of all the razor wire tomorrow . . . if there weren't so many immigrants around.'

'Oh?'

'It used to be the Poles, now it's Romanians and Bulgarians, I believe. I'm the last person to be racist, but . . .' And as Phoebe Braithwaite's rant continued, Jude wondered how many times Josie Achter had heard similar sentences started like that. She wasn't part of the latest influx from Romania and Bulgaria; she belonged to a race that had arrived in the British Isles many centuries before. But maybe Josie's allegations of anti-Semitism in Fethering weren't so far off the mark, after all.

Jude came out of her reverie to hear Phoebe continuing, '. . . steal anything that's not nailed down. Do you know, some Romanian youths actually tried to steal that dinghy down the garden only a few weeks back.'

'Oh, did you see them doing it?'

'No.'

Then how, Jude was tempted to ask, did you know that they were Romanian? Or youths, come to that?

'But there was no doubt there'd been a break-in. Quintus found the evidence the following morning. They'd used wire-cutters to get through the chain that holds the gates together and they'd definitely been messing about with the dinghy.'

'But it was still there, was it?'

'Oh yes. Though Quintus wondered whether the youths might

have actually taken it out during the night and rowed it about in the sea.'

'Why would they do that?'

'Sheer vandalism. That's what happens if you grow up in a country that has no respect for property. Places like Romania and Bulgaria may not still be called communist states, but that's what they are. And the communists have never had any respect for property.'

Jude had a feeling that what was being quoted at her were the undiluted opinions of Commodore Braithwaite. She looked down to the end of the garden to the blue rowing boat under discussion.

'Anyway, that morning, when Quintus inspected the dinghy, he found there was water and some shingle in it. He was convinced the youths had actually taken it on the sea during the night.'

'Well,' Jude said with a grin, 'at least they had the good manners to bring the boat back.'

'Huh,' said Phoebe, who clearly didn't believe that any excuses should be made for the Romanian youths (or whoever actually broke into Hiawatha's garden).

'And when did you say this was?' asked Jude. 'A few weeks back?'

'I remember exactly when it was, because Quintus and I had just come back from visiting one of our sons who's at university in St Andrews. We arrived back late on the Saturday, the third. So Quintus found that the boat had been tampered with on the morning of the Sunday. Sunday the fourth of October.'

Jude didn't show any outward sign of the impact that Phoebe Braithwaite's words had had on her. The fourth of October was, of course, her birthday.

Not only that, it was also the morning that Sara Courtney had found no sign in Polly's store room of the corpse she had seen there the previous night.

A corpse which might have been rowed out to sea, had weights tied to its legs and then been dropped off the side of a small boat.

EIGHTEEN

The launch for the new incarnation of Polly's Cake Shop had been scheduled for the Saturday before Christmas. Some members of the Action Committee, including Jude (who still hadn't managed to get off the bloody thing) and Arnold Bloom (who saw it as his mission in life to oppose any proposal made by Quintus Braithwaite), had been of the opinion that this was not a good date, because everyone would be scurrying about preparing for the festive season and wouldn't have time to spend drinking free coffee and eating free cupcakes.

But they were overruled by the Commodore, whose view was that Fethering Parade was never fuller than in the weeks before Christmas. Also there would be a bonhomous Christmas Spirit in the air, which could only help to make the launch a joyous occasion. And given the media blitz that Lesley Tarquin was going to unleash about the event, soon no one in West Sussex would be unaware of Polly's Cake Shop's resurrection.

It had also been agreed by the SPCS Action Committee that Polly's Cake Shop would be closed from the Monday before the launch for 'necessary refurbishment'. And Lesley Tarquin had had the idea of having 'a mega-countdown' sign on the door, starting on the Monday with 'FIVE DAYS TO REOPENING', and building to 'REOPENING TOMORROW' on the Friday. There would be lots of streamers and lametta and balloons for the Saturday, and every visitor would have a 'WELCOME TO POLLY'S COMMUNITY CAFÉ' badge stuck on them on arrival. Lesley knew 'some really good places in London that do that kind of party/event stuff'.

When Jude passed on this information to Carole, it was greeted by a predictable blast of cold air. Being a grandmother twice over had not diluted her cynicism about certain things. '"Christmas Spirit"?' she'd echoed derisively. 'If Christmas Spirit does exist at all, there's certainly no evidence of it in the weeks running up to the event. Everyone stressed to bits, pressured into excessive purchasing of presents, anxious about all the cooking that will have to be done, and paranoid at the prospect of having to spend a fixed sentence of time with relatives they can't stand.'

Good old Carole, Jude had thought, she can always be relied on to cast a wet blanket over any potential ignition of jollity. But as Christmas – and the relaunch – drew nearer, Jude found she was developing more sympathy with her neighbour's views. Scrooge ruled in High Tor and Woodside Cottage.

Since her encounter with Phoebe in the kitchen of Hiawatha, Jude had had no further calls from the woman. Her Volunteer Rota was undoubtedly being worked out, but she had got the message loud and clear that Jude had no wish to be a part of it, a decision which, undoubtedly, all of her Joannas and Samanthas would have supported.

In the run-up to the relaunch a predictable ritual had been played out between the two neighbours. As soon as the date was fixed, Jude mentioned it to Carole and got the huffy response that: 'I've got better things to do with my time than go to that kind of event.' So the subject wasn't mentioned again until Carole herself raised it in a casual way. 'What was the date when they're going to do the relaunch of Polly's Cake Shop?'

Jude had told her and then asked, 'Why, were you thinking of coming?'

'Oh, good heavens, no. Just wondering when it was supposed to be happening. Because I haven't seen any publicity for it locally.'

'Don't worry, you will soon. We have a publicity officer on the committee, fresh from a London PR job, who is going to "carpet-bomb the punters". Soon everyone in the southeast will know about the launch.'

Carole sniffed. In her view all publicity was evidence of the trait that her parents always discouraged in her – 'showing off'.

'Are you sure you don't want to come?' Jude asked mischievously.

'No, of course I don't. I may be in Fulham looking after Chloe that weekend.'

'Ah. Fine.'

But as the relevant weekend approached, it turned out that Carole's services would not be required in Fulham. So, with characteristic lack of grace, she said to Jude that she 'might come along to Polly's, just to see what kind of a mess they'd made of the place'.

By the Friday, the day before the launch, Carole Seddon was

positively excited about what she was going to see in Polly's Cake Shop – or, as it was now called, Polly's Community Café. She also felt good because she reckoned she had finally tracked down perfect Christmas presents for both Lily and Chloe.

The impression they had, on entering the premises for the relaunch (and having their 'WELCOME TO POLLY'S COMMUNITY CAFÉ' badges stuck on), was of considerable change. During the five days of the café's closure, the rough white plaster of the walls had been smoothed down and painted a duck-egg blue. The red and white gingham table cloths had been replaced by ones in French navy, and the horse brasses and warming pans hanging from the beams had given way to impressionistic splurges of local seascapes. 'Done by this wonderful little woman we know,' Phoebe Braithwaite explained later. '*So* talented. We bought all the pictures from her outright, which means we can sell them to customers – who I'm sure will just *love* them – and then all the money we make will of course go straight into Polly's funds.'

Whereas the previous décor of the café had had a distinct retro style of the 1940s, its new incarnation seemed to Carole stranded in time, not fussy enough to be archaic nor yet minimalist enough to be modern. Jude had similar views, and also wondered how much of Kent Warboys' twenty grand had been eaten up by the refurbishment. 'At first,' Phoebe Braithwaite explained later, 'we had thought of getting together a huge community group to strip the place down and do the redecoration ourselves. But wiser counsels prevailed and we decided we didn't want to spoil the café for a ha'porth of tar and it would be cheaper to get in a professional to do the job. And we've got this wonderful little man who's done all the decorating work at Hiawatha and . . .' Jude also wondered how much that had cost.

But the expense of the decorating must have been small beer compared to that of the new costumes for the waitresses. Gone were the black and white uniforms of Agatha Christie adaptations (and popular sexual fantasies), which had toned so well with the previous retro style. In their place, Phoebe Braithwaite's cohort of Joannas or Samanthas were wearing short-skirted tunics in French navy, on the front of which were embroidered the anchor and cannon motif which had distinguished Quintus Braithwaite's notepaper. 'We

wanted a completely fresh look,' Phoebe Braithwaite explained later.
'And I know this wonderful little woman in London who runs up
stuff like that on an absolute shoestring. She's done so many "special
occasion" dresses for me. Her own original designs are but so, so
economical.'

Jude again wondered how much of Kent Warboys' twenty grand
was left.

She overheard Phoebe responding to compliments on the café's
new look. 'Well, I think it's very important that we take the place
a bit upmarket. The Seaview Café on the beach is always there for
day-trippers and people from the Downside estate. We want Polly's
to have a bit more *cachet* . . .'

It was hard to discover what the format of the relaunch was. The
people of Fethering, all intrigued to inspect the makeover, drifted
in to be fed coffee and cupcakes. Phoebe Braithwaite's blue-liveried
Joannas or Samanthas were very efficient at serving these. The café's
Italian coffee machine did not present any problems for them – they
all had much more advanced versions in their own kitchens. And
serving a cupcake on a plate with a doily on it was not rocket
science. 'Just for the launch,' Phoebe Braithwaite explained later,
'we did buy in the cupcakes. Of course we'll bake everything on
site when the café's up and running. But with all the decorating
going on, it was difficult to get into the kitchen at Polly's. And I
do know this very clever little woman in Brighton who does the
most splendid bakery of all kinds. And I thought having the words
"Welcome to Polly's Community Café" in icing on them was a
justifiable expense . . . as a one-off for this very special occasion.
And also I thought it'd be good publicity . . . you know, a photo
of one of the cupcakes in the local press – or, even better, on the
telly-box – would be just massive free publicity.'

For the relaunch Polly's doors had opened at ten thirty. Tasteful
Vivaldi played in the background, though it was soon inaudible
against the clash of voices. Phoebe's Volunteer Rota of Joannas or
Samanthas were squeakily loud in their high-pitched chatter, and
their husbands, all dressed in crushed strawberry corduroy trousers
and quilted khaki gilets, brayed constant hilarities to each other.
The locals, as usual, exchanged the latest Fethering gossip.

One person who hoped to be conspicuous by his absence was
Arnold Bloom. He boycotted the relaunch as an expression of his

protest against the changing of the café's name. But, sadly for him, nobody noticed he wasn't there.

A long time elapsed before it became clear whether there was going to be any focus for the morning's activities. Or was everyone just going to sit around all morning sipping coffee and eating expensively iced cupcakes? Eventually it was established that Quintus Braithwaite would be saying a few words of welcome at twelve noon. Having heard enough of his oratory to last a lifetime, Jude didn't feel tempted to stay that long.

The one thing there was no sign of amongst the throng of cupcake-munchers was a strong media presence. Certainly no sign of television cameras, not even radio reporters with microphones. And among the guests whom Carole and Jude did not recognize, none had the looks – or indeed the notebooks – of press reporters.

They were close enough to hear a rather fretful Quintus raise this issue with his publicity officer and to hear the reply from Lesley Tarquin, dressed for the occasion in purple leggings, orange baseball boots and a dress that appeared to be made of lametta. Apparently Vince at the *Fethering Observer* had started his Christmas break early and nobody from the *West Sussex Gazette* or *Sussex Life* was interested. Jezza from FOAM FM was tied up with a Secret Santa Charity Foam-Fight, Will at Radio Solent was hosting a Twenty-Four-Hour Christmas Carol-a-Thon, and Flick at Radios Surrey and Sussex hadn't got back to her, in spite of . . .

Jude caught Carole's eye. 'Shall we slip away to the pub?' she said.

The Crown and Anchor would fill up later with weary shoppers whose Christmas spirit was already draining away, but at half past eleven when Carole and Jude got there they were among the first customers. Zosia, who was in charge of the bar, greeted them warmly and, without waiting for an order, poured two large glasses of New Zealand Sauvignon Blanc.

Carole said instinctively, 'Oh, surely it's a bit early in the day to be—?'

'We've earned it,' Jude interrupted. 'A reward for surviving that scrum at Polly's.'

'Well, I just thought that maybe . . .' And with that Carole's objections trickled away.

As they moved across to their regular alcove, someone called out

Jude's name. She looked across to the source of the sound and saw the waitress Binnie Swales and the chef Hammo whom she'd met with Sara Courtney at Polly's some weeks before. Both had pints of Guinness in front of them.

'I see you were there then,' Binnie continued accusingly.

Jude couldn't think what was meant until, looking down at her coat, she saw the 'WELCOME TO POLLY'S COMMUNITY CAFÉ' was still stuck there. Carole, needless to say, had removed hers at the first opportunity after they'd left the café.

'Yes, we were there,' Jude admitted. 'Were you not invited?'

'God, no.' Binnie chuckled. 'We would have lowered the tone far too much. We're never going to fit in with Phoebe Braithwaite's Bitch Brigade, are we?'

'What about Sara?' Jude suddenly remembered she hadn't seen her at the relaunch.

'She wasn't invited either.'

'Besides,' said Hammo sarcastically, 'having people there who actually know how to run a café . . . well, that would have spoiled the image, wouldn't it?'

Jude chuckled wryly. 'Oh, this, by the way, is my friend Carole.'

Carole flashed a short smile at them and was set to continue to their alcove. On the whole she tried to avoid meeting Jude's friends – they too often turned out to be rather flaky, New Age people. But she got more interested when Jude said the two in the pub worked at Polly's Cake Shop. 'Or should that be – "used to work at Polly's Cake Shop"?'

'No, we're still there,' replied Binnie. She was wearing a fiercely yellow cardigan and green trousers decorated with a design of large red peonies. Hammo had on jeans and a dark hoodie.

'Oh yes,' Hammo agreed. 'Working out our notice.'

'Ah.'

'Do join us,' offered Binnie, pushing back into her bun some grey hair that had escaped. Jude's eyes checked quickly with Carole's and received permission so they sat down at Binnie and Hammo's table.

'Working out your notice?' Jude picked up.

'Yes, just a month,' Binnie replied. 'We were told last week. Means we'll be out of a job in the middle of January.'

'Which is just about the worst possible time of year in the catering business,' said Hammo. 'Everyone takes on extra staff running up to Christmas, then they let them all go after New Year's Eve. So there's lots of people out there looking for jobs, and business is such crap during January and February that no one's hiring.'

'No,' Binnie agreed. 'I've worked in a lot of the local pubs and they never take on anyone in January. Used to be a regular behind the bar of the Fethering Yacht Club – nice easy job that was, did it for years – but there's someone else who's got her feet under the table there now. I'm never going to get another job at my age.'

'So you're neither of you keen on the concept of Polly's Community Café?' asked Carole.

'You could say that.' Hammo grinned wryly. 'I'd tend to use stronger language, but not in the company of three ladies.'

'Your delicacy is appreciated,' said Jude. 'But you've made me feel rather guilty. I did raise the issue at committee of what would happen to the existing staff, but the meeting moved on to other topics. I'm sorry I should have pursued it further. I didn't think through the ramifications.'

'You are not alone,' said Hammo, 'in not having thought through the ramifications. I am extremely . . .' he was about to use a stronger word but curbed the instinct '. . . extremely annoyed about it. Just moved down from "the Smoke" to Littlehampton six months ago with the girlfriend and the little one. Got a flat. And a mortgage. So you are right. I am less than enthused about Polly's Cake Shop becoming a Community Project.'

'Don't you have any legal redress?'

Hammo shook his head and Binnie explained, 'Our contracts specify a month's notice on either side. Josie Achter wasn't the friendliest of bosses, but at least she was straight. And I'd known for a while that she was thinking of selling up, so I thought that'd just mean a new boss and everything would continue working in just the same way. Never occurred to me that the place would be taken over by the *community*.' The distaste with which she spoke the word was worthy of Carole.

'If it's any comfort,' said Jude, 'I don't think the café will run for very long as a Community Project.' What she'd seen at the morning's launch did not suggest that the new venture was on a very sound financial footing. 'Initiatives like that do have a habit of coming unstuck quite quickly.'

'Not quickly enough for us,' said Binnie gloomily. 'So I'm afraid no, Jude, it's not any comfort.'

'Of course,' said Carole, 'it'll be the same for your friend too, won't it?'

'Which friend?' asked Jude, not very quick on the uptake.

'Sara Courtney. She'll be out of a job too, won't she?'

Binnie snorted derisively. 'Don't you worry about her. She'll be all right.'

'Oh?'

'Got this new boyfriend, hasn't she?'

Hammo was incensed by the reminder. 'Only the bastard who's shafted us, isn't he? Kent Bloody Warboys! Oh, don't you worry about Sara. She'll be all right with Kent Warboys paying her bills.'

Jude wondered whether that was true. Until her mental breakdown, Sara had been a very self-reliant woman, always running her own businesses. She wouldn't take kindly to the idea of being a kept woman. But it wasn't worth raising that with Binnie and Hammo in their current mood.

Carole suddenly realized that, in the context of their decelerating investigation into Amos Green's death, she was in the presence of two potentially valuable witnesses. Still rather miffed that Jude hadn't told her earlier about Sara Courtney's sighting of the body in Polly's Cake Shop, she felt she had some catching up to do. And now she was being presented with the perfect opportunity to do it.

'Going off at something of a tangent,' she said, 'you two presumably heard about Jude and me finding a body on the beach?'

'Of course we did,' said Binnie. 'Come on, we do live in Fethering. Round here everyone knows if an empty suntan-cream bottle is found on Fethering Beach, let alone a dead body.'

'So did the police talk to you about it?'

Both Binnie and Hammo looked puzzled. 'Why should they?' asked Binnie.

Of course. Only Sara herself, Jude and now Carole knew what had been found in the store room. 'Sorry, I gathered they'd talked to everyone locally.'

'Not everyone.'

'No, obviously not everyone. But I thought they might have come to Polly's, you know, being a social centre of the village, to see if anyone there recognized the man.'

'Well, they didn't,' said Hammo.

When she thought about it, Carole realized that this made sense. The police of course were in that great majority of people who were unaware of any connection between Amos Green and Polly's Cake Shop.

'Mind you,' said Binnie Swales, 'if they had asked, I could have told them a thing or two.'

'Oh? Do you mean you recognized the man?'

'When his photo was on the front of the *Fethering Observer*, oh yes, I recognized him.'

'What, had you known him a long time?'

'No. Only saw him the once.'

'When was that?' asked Jude.

'Saturday, a couple of months back.'

'Would that have been the third of October?'

Binnie did a quick calculation. 'Yes, you're right.'

'And where did you see him?'

'In Polly's. He ordered a large Americano. Very charming he was; had a way with him. One of those men who can make a woman feel not quite so old for a moment or two.'

'Did you see him too, Hammo?' asked Carole.

The chef shook his head. 'Busy in the kitchen, wasn't I?'

'Did he say anything to you, Binnie? Apart from the compliments, that is.'

'Yes. When he paid his bill – and he tipped a whole quid, which is a lot for an Americano, even a large one – he asked if Josie Achter was around.'

'But she wasn't.'

'No, I told him she was in Brighton. I gave him her mobile number – and Rosalie's. Thought he might be able to track her down.'

'But you don't know whether he did or not?'

'No idea.'

NINETEEN

Unfortunately that seemed to be the full extent of Binnie's information. Having been told that Josie was in Brighton for the day, Amos Green had left Polly's Cake Shop. Where he went next, nobody knew. Whether he then met the person who shot him in some prearranged venue, or returned to Polly's to be murdered there, were questions that raised considerable frustration in Carole and Jude.

Before Christmas intervened they did make a couple of investigation-related phone calls. Jude rang the flat above the café, hoping to make contact with Josie Achter, but only got an answering machine. Later in the day she got a response to her message from Rosalie. Her mother was not in a rented flat, she was in a hotel in Hove. She didn't want Rosalie to tell anyone which hotel and she had just changed the number of her mobile phone. The meaning was pretty clear – Josie Achter did not wish to be contacted, least of all by anyone from Fethering.

'It's just,' said Jude, 'in connection with the body that was found on Fethering Beach.'

'Oh?' asked Rosalie. 'In what way?'

'On the afternoon of Saturday the third of October, the dead man was actually seen in Polly's Cake Shop.'

'Was he?' Rosalie Achter's voice was bleached of all emotion. 'Do the police know that?'

'Apparently not.'

'Hm. Are you going to tell them?

'Don't feel any great urgency to.'

'I'm glad to hear it.'

'Why do you say that, Rosalie?'

'Oh, I got into a bit of trouble with the police while I was a student. Let's just say I don't have a very high opinion of them and certainly wouldn't go out of my way to give them any help.'

'Gotcha.'

'Who is your witness, though? Who saw him in Polly's?'

Instinctive caution made Jude reply, 'I don't think that's important.'

'I think it could be very important.'

'Perhaps. My contacting your mother about it could also be important.'

'What do you mean, Jude? What game are you playing?'

And Jude realized that she was playing a game. Which was out of character for her. Normally she went at things directly. But having started on this unfamiliar route, she pursued it. 'I was just thinking, Rosalie . . . I would trade you the name of my witness . . . for your mother's new mobile number.'

'Forget it!' said Rosalie Achter. And the phone was slammed down.

Carole and Jude did briefly discuss whether they should pass on their new information to Janice Green. 'But she was so adamant about wanting that chapter of her life closed,' said Carole.

'Yes. Alternatively she did suggest we give any new information we get to the police.'

'Yes, yes.' Carole was torn between the principles which had been inculcated into her at the Home Office and her natural instinct for secrecy. 'I suppose we should.'

'On the other hand,' said Jude, letting her friend off the hook, 'it'd be a bit rotten for Binnie to have the police hassling her, wouldn't it?'

'Absolutely,' said Carole with gratitude. 'You're right.'

And then Christmas intervened. And though Jude had hoped for a low-key celebration, spending the inside of 'The Big Day' with some friends in Hastings, there still seemed to be a lot of preparations that required making. And a lot of clients who needed alternative therapy to strengthen them for the invasion of uncongenial relatives which lay ahead.

For Carole, always a bit wary that Christmas would draw attention to the essential loneliness of her life, this year was different. She had been asked by Stephen and Gaby to come up to Fulham on Christmas morning and to stay until Boxing Day evening. This would mean spending the best part of two days with her pair of beautiful grandchildren. Though she wouldn't have admitted it to anyone, Carole was chuffed to bits at the prospect.

* * *

In the few days running up to Christmas, Polly's Cake Shop did a roaring trade. Phoebe Braithwaite's Volunteer Rota worked an absolute treat, and the many locals who went to check out the new facilities were delighted by the efficient (and rather classier than before) service provided by the Joannas or Samanthas in their trim French navy tunics.

Hammo, working out his notice, was as efficient as ever – and generously helpful too in showing the volunteers who'd be taking over from him how everything worked. Binnie, however (who Phoebe Braithwaite thought did not suit the new image for Polly's waitresses), was delegated to work out her notice washing up out of sight in the kitchen. Though she made no visible demur at this demotion, people who knew Binnie Swales well would recognize exactly how much she was seething beneath her placid exterior.

And Sara Courtney hadn't been seen in Polly's Cake Shop since the relaunch.

So Jude was only slightly surprised when, the day after Boxing Day, she had a call from her. 'I'm sorry, Jude. I've got this terrible back pain.'

'But mentally okay?'

'Yes . . . yes,' came the uncertain reply. 'Pretty much.'

'All still good with Kent?'

'Yes. Very good. We spent Christmas together. With his kids as well. And I met his ex-wife briefly when she handed them over.'

Jude hadn't known that Kent was a father. Or a divorcé. But few men were going to get to Kent Warboys' age without carrying the baggage of some marriage or long-term relationship. Jude reckoned she knew what had caused the tension in Sara Courtney's back. They made an appointment for the next day, the Thursday.

Her client's back was very tense, but Jude could feel the tightness was already going. The stress which had caused the pain arose from seeing Kent Warboys' wife and spending time with his children. It had been quite a lot to ask of Sara so early into their relationship. Now that she was no longer in their presence, the tension was draining naturally out of her.

As a result the treatment required did not really call on Jude's healing skills. It was just a basic back massage. And once it was completed, Sara felt instantly better.

Jude made them both a cup of green tea. Then she said,

'Incidentally, I had some corroboration for what you saw on the third of October.' Sara looked confused. 'Amos Green. He was seen, still very much alive, in Polly's that afternoon.'

'Oh. Was he?'

'So, while not exactly being proof that you saw his dead body, it does at least link him to the site where you found it.'

'Yes, I suppose so.'

'Binnie saw him in the café. She served him an Americano.' Jude had no inhibition about naming her source to Sara.

'Oh, did she?' There wasn't a lot of interest in the words. 'I have, incidentally, decided that I did definitely see the body. It wasn't a hallucination.'

'And what made you decide that? More proof?'

'No, nothing like that. I'm just mentally in so much better a place that I can tell reality from hallucination. And what I saw in that store room was real.'

'Good. I'm glad your confidence has come back.' There was a silence. 'Does this mean that you're thinking of going to the police about what you saw?' A firm shake of the head. 'Why not?'

'For the reason I just told you. I'm mentally in so much better a place that I don't want to threaten my new-found mental equilibrium by getting involved in police interviews.'

Carole might not have approved, but it was a good enough answer for Jude. 'And have you still got your one piece of solid proof? The handkerchief with Amos Green's blood on it?'

'Yes. I've kept thinking of throwing it away, but every time something stops me.'

Jude didn't comment on this but was secretly pleased. She had a feeling that that piece of evidence might at some stage prove vital to the investigation. The thought prompted another: that what she and Carole were doing hardly qualified for the title of an 'investigation'. Though they had assembled a number of tantalizing details, their enquiries were lacking a sense of forward momentum. She wondered if it was just because Christmas had put everything on hold, but she was rather afraid that wasn't the reason. The case was just slipping away from them.

She grinned at Sara. 'Anyway, I'm glad to hear that everything's going well with Kent. And that you've come through the baptism of fire.'

'What do you mean?'

'Meeting his ex-wife and children.'

'Ah. Yes. Well, you're right. It was quite stressful.'

'So your back told me.'

Sara chuckled. 'I have a very articulate back.'

'You certainly do. So . . . with Kent in place . . . there are no clouds on your horizon?'

'Fewer clouds, anyway.'

'How do you mean?'

Sara grimaced. 'Well, the fact is . . . yes, with Kent things're going fine. Better than I ever imagined things going with a man. Certainly better than they were with the last one.'

'Not difficult, from what you've said about him.'

'No, you're right. Now it seems incongruous that I stayed with him so long; that I actually wanted to have children with him. It's amazing how volatile we are, how we can totally convince ourselves of the rightness of something that is so obviously wrong. I do find human nature confusing.'

'I think we all do.'

'Hm. Anyway, so as regards my love life, no clouds on my horizon.' Thinking perhaps this was too bold an assertion, she backtracked a little. 'Well, no clouds at the moment. Probably some will come floating by soon.'

'No reason why they should. Some things in life just work.'

'Sadly that hasn't been my experience too often.'

'But your life is changing.'

'Hope so.' The grin that accompanied these words twisted itself into a grimace. 'It's my work life that's not so good, though. Well, nonexistent. And that does frustrate me. I've been working for myself ever since I left school. And not having a project of my own to concentrate on is really getting me down.'

'I see that Binnie and Hammo are working out their notice at Polly's.'

'Yes. And you're wondering why I'm not doing the same . . .?'

'Had crossed my mind, yes.'

'I'll tell you why. Because Phoebe Braithwaite is the rudest woman I have ever met!'

'Ah.'

'She made no secret of the fact that she thought I ought to forgo my earnings during my month's notice. She said, "It's different for Binnie and Hammo – they're ordinary working people. But you're a different class from them. You should be taking part in this Community Project, not leaching away funds from it. If you are still keen to work here, then I can put you on my Volunteer Rota." "Unpaid?" I asked. "Of course unpaid," she replied. "That's what 'volunteer' means. Don't you have any sense of community?" And I'm afraid that was when I really lost my rag.'

'I'm not surprised.'

'I told her I had always earned my own living, and my hands-on experience in the catering business meant that I was extremely highly qualified. And nobody was going to get the advantage of my skills for free. Then she had the nerve to say, "I don't know why you're getting so het up about it. Now you're shacked up with Kent Warboys, it's not as if you need to work." Well, that did it. I stormed out – and will probably never go into Polly's Cake Shop again!'

'I can understand that,' said Jude.

'But at the same time,' said Sara, quickly calming down, 'I'm quite sorry about that.'

'Oh?'

'I really enjoyed working at Polly's. Even under Josie. She wasn't the most friendly of employers, but she recognized what I could do. She kept giving me more responsibility. I think I could have ended up managing the place . . . if this bloody Community Project hadn't come along.'

'And is this a source of friction between you and Kent? Because, after all, he's been a great supporter of running Polly's as a Community Project.'

'So far we've managed to keep off the subject.'

'Long may that last.'

'You betcha. I'm not going to threaten the best relationship I've ever had by arguing over Polly's Cake Shop. No, once everyone has gone back to work after the long Christmas break, I will seriously set about the business of finding myself a job.'

Jude couldn't let it alone. 'And you're still not planning to tell the police about what you saw?'

'I've told you, no. And in fact now I have a much stronger reason to keep what I saw to myself.'

'Oh?'

'It wouldn't just be me who'd get caught up in the police questioning.'

'Really? Then who?'

'Kent told me he used to know Amos Green.'

TWENTY

The decision had been taken that Polly's Community Café would not open during the long Christmas break, and this was generally thought to be a good idea. Though most of Fethering's residents and a lot of the village's weekenders would be around over the holiday, most of them would be staying in their homes. It made sense for the café's Volunteer Rota to enjoy their own Christmases and then reopen in the New Year with refreshed energy.

It was on the morning before New Year's Eve, the Sunday, that Jude had a panicked call from Carole asking if she could look after Gulliver. She'd just had a call from Fulham. Her new granddaughter Chloe had been rushed into hospital with a respiratory problem. Granny's services were required to look after Lily.

Jude could hear how terrified her neighbour was and she knew the reason. Memories of her own stillborn second child had made Chloe seem particularly vulnerable to Carole. She still had a terrible fear of history repeating itself.

But of course Carole didn't mention this on the phone. And Jude was far too sensitive and diplomatic to raise the subject herself. She just rushed straight round to High Tor to take charge of Gulliver while Carole, uncharacteristically slapdash, threw some clothes into a bag and drove off in the Renault at a pace far beyond the sedate speed limit of Fethering. Jude had made her promise to let her know when there was any news of Chloe.

Gulliver seemed quite content to snuffle around the unfamiliar smells of Woodside Cottage. Carole hadn't got the message from Fulham until after she and the dog had returned from Fethering Beach, so he wouldn't need another walk till the late afternoon.

Jude had a couple of clients booked in that morning (more refugees from tense family Christmases) and she didn't think either of them would object to the dog's presence during their sessions. She was removing its disguise of throws and cushions and assembling her treatment bed when the phone rang.

It was Kent Warboys. 'I wondered if we could have a chat, Jude.'

'Yes, of course. About anything in particular?'

'About Sara. I'm worried about her.'

The arrangement that they had made was that Jude would go to Kent's home late afternoon and use the excursion for Gulliver's second walk of the day. The architect lived on the opposite bank of the Fether estuary from the Fethering Yacht Club. Only a few hundred yards away. But getting to his house involved walking back up the towpath to the last road bridge before the sea and then walking back on the other side. The few hundred yards as the crow flies became a mile, a perfect workout for Gulliver.

Kent Warboys' house was a conversion from some old fishermen's huts, which had been about to collapse when he'd bought them, and they provided a very good sales pitch for the kind of sympathetic development on which Warboys Heritage Construction prided itself. Though the building had every state-of-the-art modern amenity, it still retained the outline of its former usage and looked as if it had always stood there at the junction of the Fether and the English Channel.

Just before she rang the doorbell, Jude checked again with her mobile. There was no message from Fulham. Disquiet within her grew.

Kent was very welcoming when he let her and Gulliver in and led them to an upstairs sitting room whose windows, filling one whole wall, commanded stunning views over the sea. The weather outside might have been icy cold, but the interior was very cosy. Jude could see no sign of a fireplace, stove or radiators. No doubt the building was warmed by the latest unseen heating technology.

Kent offered her a drink and asked if he could get some water for Gulliver. 'Used to have a Lab myself, know how thirsty they can get.'

Jude accepted the offer on the dog's behalf and said she'd like a glass of white wine. Kent had a bottle of New Zealand Sauvignon Blanc in the fridge, which was perfect. He poured himself a Becks beer.

'Thanks so much for coming over,' he said.

'No problem. You say you're worried about Sara . . .?'

'Yes. And I know she's been to see you about some of the . . . problems she's had in the past—'

'She has, but—'

'I know, I know. She's one of your clients and I understand that – like anyone involved in medicine – you have a duty of client confidentiality.'

'Yes, I do.'

'So I wouldn't dream of asking you to tell me about secrets she might have confided in you in the course of your healing sessions.'

'Thank you.' Jude was once again impressed by Kent Warboys' apparent honesty. He seemed to be genuinely thoughtful and aware of other people's sensibilities.

'But, Jude, if I tell you things that Sara has told me, then we can discuss those, can't we? No confidentiality issue there, is there?'

'No,' Jude replied cautiously.

'And look, I should start by saying that I'm really deeply serious about my relationship with Sara. I've been bowled over by her ever since I met her. And I really do want this to be something that continues – ideally forever.'

'Good. I gather that she's pretty serious too.'

'I hope so. She says so. And I know things were a bit sticky for her over Christmas. My fault. I went too fast. Shouldn't have brought the kids and the ex-wife into the equation so early. But I think she pulled through okay.'

'I got that impression, yes.'

'I'm glad to hear it. But listen, Jude, I know from things Sara has told me that she has recently had a fairly major breakdown.'

'Yes, she has.'

'But she's coming out of it and she's feeling a lot more positive. And I think a lot of that is down to the sessions you've been doing with her.'

Jude shrugged. 'I hope I've helped. Most of it is down to her, though. She's worked stuff out for herself.'

'Mm.' Kent paused for a moment and took a long swig of his beer. Gulliver panted contentedly on the carpet. 'What I really want to know, Jude, is how strong Sara is . . .?'

'Strong for what?'

'For going back to work.'

'Well, she's been working at Polly's until quite recently.'

'Yes, but just as a waitress. Way below her skill level. And she was getting very frustrated by it. Sara has run her own restaurant for years, after all. And she wants to get back into some kind of managerial role, which is quite honestly where she belongs. But I'm just wondering whether she is strong enough to be applying for jobs of that kind.'

'I'd say it was up to her. If Sara thinks she can cope, then I'm sure she can cope.'

'Hm.' Kent's tone didn't make it sound as if Jude had resolved the problem to his full satisfaction. 'It's just . . . when she describes the kind of state she was in – you know, hallucinating, seeing things that weren't there . . .'

'It's not an unusual symptom of stress, and she had been suffering from a very high level of stress.'

'Yes. If I were ever to meet that bastard, her ex-boyfriend, well, I don't think I'd be responsible for my actions.' Kent Warboys spoke with a rather frightening cold passion that Jude hadn't heard from him before.

'Let's hope you don't meet him then.'

'Right.' But there was a tinge of regret in his voice. Then he moved on. 'I'm fortunate. I've never had any kind of mental illness. You know, I've had my frustrations in my professional life. When you run a company, the bigger the scale of the operation, the more problems you get.'

'Are you talking about Warboys Heritage Construction?'

'No, that's a relatively new company for me, and now I'm a bit cannier about how to run things. There have been so many companies over the years, though, most of which have had to be wound up at some point.'

'Why?'

'Oh, the usual reasons – cash-flow problems, bankrupt subcontractors, clients who refuse to pay, unreliable partners, criminal partners, you name it. My first company was called Warboys Design and Build, then I was Fit The Build for a while; terrible name – my then partner's choice, not mine, I hasten to add. Then I was . . . Anyway, none of this is important. I was talking about how lucky I am never to have been depressed. So yes, there have been frustrations in my professional life, and in my personal life too, come to that – but they've just made me bloody angry. Never depressed, never not trusting my own eyes as to whether what I'm seeing is real or not. The way Sara describes it . . . God, it's scary.'

'It is, yes.'

'Have you ever . . .?'

Jude shook her head. 'But I've seen enough evidence of the misery it can cause.'

'I'm sure you have. Still, I think it's good that people are more open about mental illness these days.'

'I agree completely.'

'I mean nowadays you hardly ever read an interview with an actor or singer who hasn't had some kind of battle with depression.'

'It's an essential part of a contemporary showbusiness CV,' said Jude with some cynicism.

'Everything's much more transparent these days. Get your secrets out in the open: that seems to be the modern mantra, and a very good one too. Imagine, even ten years ago, the idea of same-sex marriage being legal.'

'Yes, there has been improvement in some areas,' Jude agreed cautiously.

'I mean, I'm sure you and Carole must've noticed the change.'

Jude was totally confused. 'Sorry?'

'Well, nowadays you don't get any hassle about your relationship, do you?'

Finally she caught on to what he was saying and, with difficulty avoiding giggling, replied, 'No, we don't get any hassle at all.'

From previous experience, Jude knew that there was a small element in the Fethering community who, because the two women were seen around so much together, assumed that Carole and Jude were a lesbian couple. Jude always found references to this hysterically funny. Carole was less amused.

The thought of her friend took Jude's mind to the children's ward of a hospital in Fulham. She framed a silent, nondenominational prayer for the health of Chloe Seddon.

'Mental illness is scary, though,' Kent went on. 'I mean, have you seen those scars on Sara's arms?' Jude nodded. 'How much do you have to hate yourself to start doing that? And there are other awful symptoms she's told me about. At her worst Sara claims to have seen whole scenarios that just didn't exist.' Another silence, another swig of beer. 'She told me she'd once seen a dead body.'

'Oh.'

'In Polly's – back in the day when it was still Polly's Cake Shop, not Polly's Community Café. She told me she'd seen this body of a man who'd been shot, there in the store room.'

'Did you believe her?'

'Well, no. I mean, I believed her when she told me that she'd had the hallucination. But I don't believe she'd actually seen the body, no.' He looked at Jude shrewdly. 'I suppose it wouldn't be . . . *proper* for me to ask if she'd ever mentioned that hallucination to you?'

She was quite relieved to be able to say, 'No, it wouldn't be proper.'

'I thought not.'

'Has she mentioned it recently . . . you know, seeing the body?'

'No. She only talked about it once. When she was trying to explain to me how low she felt at times. It was just when we were starting to get to know each other . . . you know, that stage when you tell your new partner the worst things about yourself, to see if it'll put them off.'

'And what Sara told you didn't put you off?'

'No, it's her I love . . . and I guess the mental fragility just comes along as part of the package.'

'Hm. And what did you tell her?'

'Sorry?'

'What were the worst things about you?'

He chuckled. 'Nothing, I'm glad to say . . . or at least nothing that put her off.' And Jude realized that was all the answer she was going to get.

So, cautiously, she moved on to another subject. 'Sara never said to you, did she, whether she recognized the body she claimed to have seen? Whether it looked like someone she knew?'

'No,' said Kent. But was Jude being hypersensitive to detect a new carefulness in his reply? Was he really unaware of the connection between the body seen in Polly's store room and the one found on Fethering Beach?

'Anyway,' he went on, 'you reckon I should encourage Sara to apply for managerial jobs? You think she's up to it?'

'I think Sara has a very shrewd estimation of her own abilities. If she reckons she's up to anything, then I'm sure she is.'

'Thank you, that's really helpful. I'm sorry to have bothered you, but I didn't really know who else to ask. There aren't that many people around who know Sara really well. She was so locked up in that relationship with the bastard restaurateur that she doesn't seem to have many friends.

'Which is actually another thing that we have in common,' Kent added.

Jude looked at him in some surprise.

'Oh, I've got any number of acquaintances, I see a lot of people in the course of my work, but I wouldn't say I have many close friends.'

'So, when you're in a relationship with someone, it tends to be very closed-in and exclusive, does it?'

'I suppose it does, really, yes.'

'Which must make things painful if it breaks up.'

'Yes, the closer a couple are, the more pain when it does end.' Kent looked at Jude as if he felt he had to defend himself. 'Look, I know you're a friend of hers, but I swear I have no intention to hurt Sara. I'm not denying I've had other relationships since the divorce where we've got very close, but it didn't work . . . you know, different priorities, age difference, women wanting children when I've already got some; all the usual reasons. But I do sincerely believe that in Sara I have finally found the right one.'

'Good.'

'And well, it's been strange, this extended Christmas break. It's a long time to spend together when a relationship's fairly new. I just hope I haven't crowded Sara, haven't been too full-on for her.' He looked a little anxious. 'And maybe that's why she insisted on going up to London to do some shopping today. Perhaps I was making her feel a bit claustrophobic. Perhaps she needed a bit of space.'

'Maybe. Mind you, I should point out that some of the January sales have started early. Even the Sunday after Christmas is quite a popular day for shopping.'

He chuckled. 'Yes, I hadn't thought of that.'

'I wouldn't worry about a thing, Kent. I'm sure the pair of you'll be fine.'

'I hope so. I sincerely hope so.'

'Well, Gulliver and I must be on our way.' Jude stood up and moved closer to the window. She looked down at the garden. It was neatly laid out and well looked after, though there wasn't much growing at that time of year.

Kent followed her eye-line. 'As you can imagine, only very hardy stuff survives down there. All the salt spray and the wind.'

'I'm sure.' She noticed there was a locked gate in the wall that led down to the beach. And, just inside it, on a light trailer, was a silver-coloured rubber dinghy.

'Do you use that much?' she asked.

'Oh, just for pottering around. My real boat's in the Fethering Yacht Club marina – or moored to the few pontoons they have the nerve to *call* a marina.'

'Hm.' Jude looked across the river mouth to the main expanse of Fethering Beach. 'It was over there, of course, that my friend Carole and I found the body of Amos Green,' she said casually.

'Yes, I heard about that.'

She turned to face him. Her brown eyes, though gentle and compassionate, could also be compelling, not to say transfixing. 'Sara told me that you knew Amos Green.'

'She told me she'd mentioned that to you. But I should say that "knew" is rather overstating the situation. I had dealings with Amos Green many years ago when I was doing some development in the Kingston area. He was on the local council there, involved in planning applications. I never knew him socially.'

'And you haven't seen him since?'

'God, no.'

'And you don't know of any connections he had with Fethering?'

'None at all,' said Kent Warboys.

TWENTY-ONE

As Jude walked Gulliver back through the afternoon chill to Woodside Cottage, her mind was full. The main question she kept asking herself was why Kent had wanted to see her. He clearly was interested in Sara's mental strength and whether she could cope with a managerial job, but at the same time that seemed to be almost a distraction. Jude got the feeling that his real purpose had been to get some other information out of her. But she couldn't for the life of her think what that information was. Or indeed whether he'd got what he wanted from her.

He'd also been extremely uncommunicative about Amos Green. Or perhaps, to put a less cynical slant on his behaviour, he had simply told her all he knew about Amos Green, and it wasn't very much. They had met professionally over some planning issue when Kent Warboys was working in the Kingston area – end of story.

But he did know that Sara had mentioned the connection to Jude. For a moment, as Gulliver pulled her resolutely homeward in expectation of his supper, she wondered if that was why Kent had wanted to see her: to check out whether she knew any more about his dealings with Amos Green. But the idea seemed tenuous.

Or was the situation even more serious? Had Kent Warboys attached himself to Sara Courtney because he'd had something to do with Amos Green's death and knew she was a kind of witness, having seen the body in the store room? Was his apparent love for her a masquerade, just a way of controlling her, to ensure that she didn't take the information she possessed to the police?

But that scenario felt far-fetched and melodramatic. And to Jude, who was a pretty good reader of human emotions, Kent Warboys' love for Sara had seemed absolutely genuine.

She wondered whether it was worth her contacting Janice Green to see if she could shed some light on the relationship between Kent and her late husband. But Jude wasn't optimistic of her enquiries getting anywhere. Janice had very firmly closed that chapter of her life.

Anyway, when she got back to Woodside Cottage there was a message on the answering machine that drove all other thoughts out of her head.

It was from Carole – absolutely characteristic of her to leave an important message on the landline. In spite of her growing love affair with computers, she was still suspicious of mobile phones. She thought they should only be used for trivia. Any really important information should be communicated on a proper phone.

It was good news. Chloe Seddon, having scared her parents and grandparent out of their wits by apparently being unable to breathe, had responded very well to the hospital treatment. The doctors' view was that she was suffering from croup, whose symptoms can be very scary to young parents witnessing them for the first time.

Chloe was being kept in hospital overnight for observation – and both her parents were going to be there with her. Carole would stay in the Fulham house, put Lily to bed and give her breakfast in the morning. The expectation was that Chloe would be discharged from the hospital after the doctor's rounds the following morning. And, if nothing else untoward had happened, Carole would be back in Fethering the following afternoon. Just in time to see the New Year in (though Carole didn't mention that – New Year's Eve was one of those dates that she just pretended wasn't in the calendar).

Jude felt hugely relieved. She also knew why Carole's message sounded so breezy and matter-of-fact. And why her neighbour had been so panicked the day before; why memories of her own loss made her so fearful for her new granddaughter. And Jude knew equally that, when they next met, that aspect of Carole's behaviour would not be mentioned.

It was a cold, slow January. Carole and Jude were reconciling themselves to the frustrating prospect of never getting any closer to unmasking the murderer of Amos Green. And, as time went by, the need to investigate became less urgent. The world was full of unsolved murders. This looked like being another one.

Meanwhile there was a lot happening at Polly's Community Café. Not a lot in the sense of a lot of customers. The bleak weather and the feeling that everyone had overspent at Christmas meant that the residents of Fethering didn't go out much. The café was nowhere near making a profit, and was being subsidized by what was left of

Kent Warboys' twenty grand. Regret was expressed in some quarters that so much had been spent on the relaunch, particularly because, in spite of Lesley Tarquin's fluent name-dropping, the event had received no press coverage whatsoever.

In mid-January Hammo and Binnie, having worked out their notice, left to test the choppy waters of the winter job market. And instantly, according to the reports of those few who did still frequent the café, standards went down, particularly in the home cooking area. When taking over as what was effectively unpaid manager, Phoebe Braithwaite had instantly cancelled all of Josie Achter's contracts with catering suppliers in Brighton. She was sure that her Volunteer Rota of Joannas or Samanthas contained some very skilled cooks – 'Quintus and I have been to some absolutely yummy dinner parties with most of them.' But whereas they might be highly skilled at spending a whole day realizing the recipes of the latest television chef sensation, few of them proved to have the abilities required by a short-order cook. Knocking up all-day breakfasts that didn't use every pan in the kitchen proved beyond the capabilities of most. The skill-sets of some of them were so iffy that even preparing beans on toast could be a challenge.

And of course in the real world Phoebe Braithwaite's Volunteer Rota was soon shown to be inadequate. Though beautifully worked out as an Excel spreadsheet on her computer (with different colours for the individual volunteers), it failed to take into account the basic rule of all human interaction – that a lot of people are extremely inefficient, and that also they change their minds.

So while all of the Joannas or Samanthas had enthusiastically filled in Phoebe's neatly printed availability lists before Christmas, when the prospect of an ongoing commitment became real they remembered all kinds of inconvenient details that had slipped their minds. A few had completely forgotten family skiing holidays that had been booked 'yonks ago'. Some had committed themselves to regular Pilates classes or volunteer reading with 'the slower ones at the local primary'. At least one had started a passionate affair with her next-door neighbour 'which is just taking up all my time'. Others had decided to focus their energies on different charitable causes which involved less of a time commitment. A good few just got bored with the whole concept of Polly's Community Café.

News of these lapses filtered through to Carole and Jude. They heard from local residents who'd found the service 'intolerably slow'. Then there were those who'd turned up at Polly's to find a notice on the door saying 'Closed due to staff shortage'.

Jude got some sense of how far down the project had declined when she received a wheedling call from Phoebe Braithwaite asking if she 'might consider stepping in to help out on a few shifts at the café . . .?' Given the way she'd been treated when her volunteering had last been discussed, Jude realized the extent to which Phoebe was scraping the barrel. She politely declined the generous offer.

All in all, what happened through January to Polly's Community Café merely reinforced the truism that there are few worse bases for a business than goodwill. When staff are being paid for doing a job they can be bawled out – or even sacked – for inefficiency. When they are volunteers, the management has no sanctions against them.

Then reports spread through the village of food poisoning. A couple of local worthies had got on the wrong side of a prawn salad in Polly's Community Café and suffered the consequences. Some careless volunteer must have left the ingredients out of the fridge too long. There was no hope of keeping the incident quiet, and it wasn't much of an advertisement for the services of the café in a place as gossipy as Fethering.

Things could not continue in that way. It was with no surprise that Jude heard the news Phoebe Braithwaite had suffered a slipped disc and was *hors de combat* as far as running the café was concerned. In the course of her healing work, Jude had seen many examples of how agonizing back pain could be. But she also knew how frequently it proved to be psychosomatic. And the timing of Phoebe's onset of agony did seem at least serendipitous.

It caused her even less surprise when an email to all of the SPCS Action Committee summoned them to another EGM at Hiawatha the following Monday.

TWENTY-TWO

'I'm afraid the figures just don't add up,' said Alec Walters in sepulchral tones. Having served as Treasurer for almost every society in Fethering, this was not the first time he had communicated such news. Most local initiatives had a very short life-span. Usually they came to an end due to the departure of their guiding light, the individual whose energy and enterprise had started the thing up. The moving-away from Fethering of such figures – or sometimes their death – was quickly followed by the demise of the project they had originated. It was rare that a replacement with comparable get-up-and-go could be found. And those who did have the requisite get-up-and-go didn't want to inherit someone else's initiative – they wanted to set up their own.

Phoebe Braithwaite's slipped disc need not have had such a terminal effect, but it was clear from her husband's attitude at the EGM that he had long since lost interest in Polly's Community Café and was looking for something else on which to focus his ego.

'Thank you for that analysis, Alec – which I have to confess doesn't surprise me. You may recall I've warned about financial problems ahead at many meetings of this committee.'

Nobody could recall him making such warnings. Chiefly because he had never made them. But nobody thought it polite to mention the fact.

'I think there comes a point,' he continued, 'in any enterprise, when you have to recognize the enemy's got the upper hand and cut your losses. In any naval engagement, a good captain is the one who knows not only when to attack, but also when to make a tactical withdrawal.'

The implication, of course, was that this observation was based on the Commodore's own experience of naval engagement, though the worst danger any of the ships he'd served had been faced with was an outbreak of swine flu.

'And I think we have probably reached that point with Polly's Community Café.'

There was an apathetic murmur of reaction from the assembled committee members, a significantly smaller number than those who had attended the previous EGM. Flora Claire, disgruntled that during its brief existence nobody had done anything about turning Polly's into a Naturopathic Health Centre, was not present. Nor was Lesley Tarquin. She had moved back up to London to resume her career in PR (with hopefully more success than she had achieved in Fethering).

There was also someone in the sitting room who shouldn't have been there. Laid out on a sofa and intermittently groaning was Phoebe Braithwaite, extracting the maximum value from her slipped disc. As a non-committee member she had no right to be present and Quintus's explanation that 'it's the only place the old thing can get comfortable' was clearly nonsense in a house the size of Hiawatha. But no one – not even Arnold Bloom – made any comment on this clear breach of committee protocol.

Jude reckoned Phoebe Braithwaite was there to inhibit criticism of her running of Polly's Community Café – and to counter any that actually did arise. Look at me, she seemed to be saying, I worked so hard on the café that I ended up with a slipped disc. She knew about the strong English aversion to hitting a man – or in this case a woman – when she was down.

'So I think it's time,' Quintus Braithwaite continued, 'to pull the plugs on Polly's Community Café. It was a splendid enterprise, into which many people – particularly my wife Phoebe – put in hard work way beyond the call of duty. But in this increasingly commercial world – given the competition from the multinational chains like Starbucks, Costa and Caffè Nero – a locally run Community Project like Polly's is bound to be up against it. So I think the best thing we can do is to close the place down – with enormous thanks to the efforts of everyone involved – and to make this the last meeting of the SPCS Action Committee.'

The majority in the room murmured lethargic agreement, but Alec Walters had a practical objection to raise. 'I'm afraid it's not quite as simple as that. The SPCS Action Committee does have a bank account – two, in fact, both current and savings accounts. And there are still funds in there, mostly what remains of Kent Warboys' generous gift of twenty thousand pounds. If the accounts are to be closed, we must make decisions on where that money should go.'

'Can't we just give it to charity?' asked Quintus dismissively.

'I think we'd need to check with Mr Warboys himself about that. Although his gift was not officially hypothecated for the running of Polly's Community Café, I think there is no doubt that that was the cause for which it was intended to be used.'

'Well, we can check that out with him.' The Commodore's attitude now was that he wanted the whole business to be finished as soon as possible.

'There is also the issue,' said Arnold Bloom, 'about what should be done with the café's other assets.'

Quintus Braithwaite was already bored with this nitpicking detail. 'All the assets of Polly's Community Café belong to Kent Warboys. He – or rather his company – owns the whole building.'

'Yes, but what's he going to do with all those tablecloths and short tunics in French navy – not mention a collection of various hideous pastiche impressionist paintings which nobody in their right mind is going to buy – and other objects on which his generous gift has been squandered?'

If it wasn't already clear that this was a direct attack on Phoebe Braithwaite's management of the café, the way Arnold looked fixedly at her left no doubt about the matter.

She groaned to remind everyone of her disabled status and said, 'I'm sure they can do some good at a charity jumble sale. In fact, there's one coming up for a charity promoting the welfare of abandoned donkeys in the Holy Land, of which Quintus has recently become the patron. They would be the perfect home for those things.'

Jude thought she now knew the cause towards which the Braithwaites' charitable energies would now be directed. One day it's a Community Café in Fethering, the next it's abandoned donkeys in the Holy Land. That seemed to fit with what she knew of Quintus and Phoebe's characters. Soon, no doubt, it'd be reopening a silted-up canal route in Blaenau Gwent or funding a classical youth orchestra in Borneo. The Braithwaites were just the kind of people who are charitable by nature.

Arnold Bloom wasn't finished yet. 'I would also like to register a very strong protest at the proposal recently put forward by the Chairman.'

'The *Chair*,' Quintus insisted.

'This committee was set up to preserve Polly's Cake Shop as a

Community Amenity for the people of Fethering. Under its current management – if that's not too positive a description of how it's been run – that ambition has not been achieved.' There was a groan from the sofa – Phoebe Braithwaite's slipped disc was really playing up. 'May I take it, Mr Chairman—?'

'*Chair.*'

'. . . that your proposal to wind up the SPCS Action Committee would incorporate your intention to resign as Chairman of the said committee?'

'Well, of course it would!' came the testy reply. 'There wouldn't be any committee for me to be Chair of, would there?'

Arnold Bloom beamed. 'In that case, I propose you submit your resignation to the SPCS Action Committee and the procedure is set in motion for the election of another Chairman.'

'But that person wouldn't have any committee to be Chair of either!'

'They would if the proposal to wind up the SPCS Action Committee were rejected.'

'What, you're suggesting that the committee should be allowed to continue to exist?'

'Yes.'

'But what possible reason could there be for that?'

'The main possible reason for that would be that . . . all right, everyone agrees that the previous approach to maintaining Polly's Cake Shop as a Community Amenity has been a complete disaster . . .' The slipped disc prompted another groan from the sofa. 'But that doesn't mean that this committee, under another Chairman and with a more businesslike approach, cannot revive the fortunes of Polly's Cake Shop.'

Quintus Braithwaite could feel the mood of the meeting turning against him. 'I resent the implication that the project has been run in an unbusinesslike way. Phoebe's Volunteer Rota was a work of pure genius.'

'Yes.' Arnold Bloom smiled, sensing he was getting the upper hand. 'But it didn't work, did it?'

'So what are you suggesting that's different?'

'I am suggesting that the café still be run basically by volunteers, but that we employ a full-time professional manager for the business.'

'You mean we *pay* someone?' The Commodore sounded thunderstruck and he received a supportive groan from the sofa. 'We can't afford that!'

'If most of the Action Committee's funds – so generously donated by Kent Warboys – hadn't been frittered away on French navy tablecloths and tunics and appalling paintings and a relaunch that failed to generate any publicity of any kind, we could easily have afforded to pay a professional manager for the last six weeks. And the place would have been run in a darned sight more efficient manner.'

'But where,' asked Quintus Braithwaite, 'are you hoping to find this paragon of all managerial virtue?'

'As a matter of fact,' said Jude, 'I know the perfect person for the job.'

TWENTY-THREE

By the end of the EGM, Arnold Bloom's triumph was complete. He had got himself elected Chairman of the SPCS Action Committee, and suggested some names 'from the local Fethering community' who might be co-opted on. Most of them were current members of the Fethering Village Committee, of which he was of course also Chairman. He suggested a date for the next meeting – on the Wednesday of that week, two days on; Arnold Bloom wasn't the kind of chairman to let the grass grow under his feet. He ordained that it – and all future meetings – should take place at All Saints Church Hall. It was agreed that Jude should sound out Sara Courtney to see if she was interested in taking the paid role of manager for Polly's Community Café. If she were, she would be invited to the Wednesday meeting to be interviewed by the renewed SPCS Action Committee.

The Braithwaites had been eclipsed completely. No refreshments were offered to the committee members departing from Hiawatha that evening (and that wasn't just because their hostess was immobilized on a sofa).

The following morning, the Tuesday, Jude received a call from Kent Warboys. 'Very good to see you over New Year.'

'My pleasure. Good to see you too.'

'Couple of things . . . One – your famous dead body.'

'Amos Green.'

'Exactly. Just wondered if the police had been in touch again . . .? You know, following up and previous questions . . .?'

'Nothing. Not a dicky bird.'

'Ah. Right. Good. Which probably means they've closed the case. So it seems likely Amos Green's death will join that massive list of "The Unexplained".'

'Looks that way, yes.'

'Hm. Anyway . . . from a rather gloomy subject to a much happier one . . . Sara and I are engaged!'

'Wonderful! That's brilliant news!'

'Certainly what we think. And we both want to thank you.'

'I haven't done anything.'

'You have. You did a lot to help Sara when she was at her lowest . . . and then to explain things to me. We're both very grateful to you.'

'Well, thank you.'

'But listen, the thing is . . . short notice and all that, but Sara and I are going to have a few drinks with some mates on Friday . . . you know, to celebrate the great event. Fethering Yacht Club, six p.m. I do hope you can come.'

'Yes, I haven't got anything else on that evening. I'd love to.'

'And do bring Carole too, if you'd like to.'

Jude bit back the giggle. 'Okay. I'll check out whether she's free.'

Needless to say, she wouldn't mention why the invitation had been issued, but she felt fairly confident that Carole would agree to come along to the yacht club. Her neighbour's inhibition about not having actually met her host and Sara as a waitress in Polly's would definitely be overcome by her ingrained nosiness.

It also struck Jude as she walked home that, given her closeness to Kent Warboys, Sara Courtney too must believe Carole and Jude were a lesbian couple, or she would have put him right about the situation. Well, the two of them had gone on holiday to Turkey together the previous year. In West Sussex such action was tantamount to announcing your same-sex marriage in the *Fethering Observer*.

Jude was still giggling when she got back to Woodside Cottage.

The subject of her sexual orientation didn't come up in the call she made to Sara shortly afterwards. After appropriate congratulations on the engagement, she said she was ringing to check out the woman's interest in the potential paid job as manager, not of Polly's Community Café, but of Polly's Cake Shop.

Sara Courtney was extremely interested. In fact, she sounded really ecstatic about the possibility. She would definitely attend the committee meeting on the Wednesday and spend the interim preparing herself for the interview. She was determined to make the job her own.

'And,' asked Jude tentatively, 'you feel confident you could cope with it?'

'At the moment, Jude,' came the sunny reply, 'I could cope with anything.'

The subject of their lesbianism was not mentioned when Jude next spoke to Carole. But she did float the suggestion that her neighbour might be interested in organizing the Volunteer Rota for the revived Polly's Cake Shop.

'That's a ridiculous idea,' came the predictable response. 'You know my views on Community Projects and volunteers.'

'Yes, but the new set-up is going to be more professional.'

'Oh?'

'The café will have a paid manager.'

'And who's that going to be?'

'Hasn't been decided yet.'

'Huh.'

'And I was just thinking,' said Jude at her most beguiling, 'that you have all that experience of organizing things at the Home Office, so I'm sure it's a job you could do.'

'The question, Jude, is not whether I could do it, but more whether I would want to do it.'

'Well, there's no hurry for you to make a decision.'

'Good.'

Jude knew from experience that this was the way things always had to be approached with her neighbour. An idea had to be proposed, agonized over and rejected a good few times before Carole would commit herself to anything.

But on this occasion, Jude could see that her interest had been engaged.

Compared to Quintus Braithwaite, Arnold Bloom was perhaps less charismatic as a Chairman (the title 'Chair' had quickly gone the way of 'Polly's Community Café'), but he was effective at working his way through an Agenda. And he was more than a match for Quintus in getting his own way.

The meeting was scheduled for seven-thirty in the All Saints Church Hall, and Sara Courtney was asked to appear at eight-fifteen for her grilling. She responded well to the questions put to her – in fact she was brilliantly charismatic. Her engagement to Kent Warboys had blown away all the cobwebs of doubt that had clouded her mind. Getting the managerial job would be icing on the cake.

Jude worried slightly about the time when Sara's volatile mood changed again, but for the moment she could only applaud her protégée's confidence.

After Sara had left the church hall, it was a matter of moments for the SPCS Action Committee to agree that she should be offered the job. As Treasurer, Alec Walters agreed to sort out and discuss with her the terms of her employment and get the appropriate contracts drawn up.

Jude said she had fixed to meet Sara in the Crown and Anchor for a drink after the meeting, and asked if she could pass on the good news.

'In fact,' Arnold Bloom replied, 'I – and many other committee members – will be adjourning to the pub, so I will be able to tell her myself. I think it would be more appropriate for such information to come from the Chairman.'

'Of course,' said Jude.

Arnold Bloom smiled with satisfaction. 'How much more convenient it is,' he observed, 'being able to go down the road to the village pub than to be dragging all the way over to some tarted-up mansion on the Shorelands Estate.'

The Fethering Yacht Club was looking surprisingly festive that evening. This was chiefly because the Christmas fairy lights round the top of the bar hadn't yet been taken down (and it was now into February). But the bar-room was a welcoming place, particularly in the winter, when all of the windows, right-angled to look over the Fether estuary and the English Channel, were closed. The glass was slick with condensation generated by the warmth of the large number of people inside.

Jude hadn't been to the yacht club since her first weeks in Fethering, when she and Carole had become involved in investigating the drowning of a boy called Aaron Spalding. But, barring the Christmas lights, not a lot seemed to have changed in the interior décor. On the wall were ships' wheels and glassed-in picture frames showing displays of nautical knots. Boards with flaking gold letters listed the club's commodores and vice-commodores, as well as the victors in various categories of sailing. In a dusty cabinet were displayed tarnished cups engraved with the names of long-dead winners.

The whole place had an air of defeat and dilapidation about it, but that didn't prevent its members from being very sniffy about who else they admitted to their ranks.

When Carole and Jude arrived that Friday evening, the engagement party was in full swing. Drink had been flowing for a while and the noise level of the conversation was high.

The affianced couple looked suitably radiant. Sara, in particular, glowed with happiness and looked wonderful in a defiantly scarlet dress. Careful make-up accentuated the sparkle of her dark eyes and her black hair was swept back into a girlish ponytail.

Kent looked good too, wearing an unflamboyant but beautifully cut suit in pale grey over a pale blue shirt. He greeted Carole and Jude effusively and directed them towards the bar 'where you can order whatever you want'. The Fethering Yacht Club did not boast a New Zealand Sauvignon Blanc, but they did have a perfectly acceptable French one (and, after all, the French had been making Sauvignon Blanc much longer than the New Zealanders).

The first people they encountered as they weaved their way back from the bar were the Braithwaites. Quintus was in blazer and crushed strawberry cords with some naval tie over his checked shirt. Phoebe was wearing rather too formal a little black dress. She moved with her customary poise.

'Delighted to see the slipped disc's getting better,' said Jude.

'Oh yes.' Phoebe Braithwaite, being Phoebe Braithwaite, showed no embarrassment about her sudden recovery. 'I've got this wonderful little man in Harley Street who's just magic with backs.'

Jude would have put money on the fact that she had been nowhere near Harley Street since the Monday meeting. She felt certain that the slipped disc, having served its purpose of getting Phoebe out of running Polly's Community Café, had neatly and conveniently slipped back to its appropriate place in its owner's spinal column.

Carole had been briefly introduced to the Braithwaites at the relaunch, and Jude was about to remind them of this when Quintus, clearly unwilling to engage in conversation, hailed a couple of yacht club acquaintances across the room and led his wife across to meet them.

Standing on the edge of the social circle, looking a little isolated, was Rosalie Achter. Carole went over to greet her. 'I think you've met my neighbour Jude.'

'I've certainly served you in the café,' said Rosalie rather brusquely. 'Served practically everyone here. Not that I'd call them my *friends*.' Jude wondered whether Rosalie had inherited some of her mother's social paranoia. 'Except perhaps Kent. Kent used to be my friend.'

'I didn't know you knew him,' said Carole.

'Ah, didn't you? No, a lot of people didn't.' This seemed a rather enigmatic reply, but Rosalie wasn't slow in providing an explanation. Her eyes, as they had been during their meeting in the Crown and Anchor, looked a little glazed. Her glass contained what looked like vodka and tonic. Once again, Carole wondered if she was a little drunk.

'What you're saying is: you wonder why I'm here.'

'Not at all. As a colleague of Sara's at the café, I—'

But Rosalie wasn't listening. 'It's a perfectly good question. I think Kent also wonders why I'm here. I was invited – Sara rang me – but I don't think Kent ever expected me to turn up. But I thought I would – just to show him.'

'Are you saying,' asked Jude tactfully, 'that there's some history between you and Kent?'

'That's a bloody tactful way of putting it, isn't it? "Some history"? Yes, we were an item. Not a full, public item,' said Rosalie sarcastically. 'Not the bells-and-whistles variety like him and Sara. No prospect of me and Kent ever having an engagement party at the Fethering Yacht Club. Sara doesn't even know that we were ever together. Oh no, I was just his "bit on the side".'

Carole looked embarrassed by her frankness. Jude now thought she understood what Kent had referred to on New Year's Eve when he mentioned 'age difference' as a reason for one of his relationships failing. And she remembered Carole reporting that Rosalie had been with someone but broken up four months previously. The news opened up a lot of intriguing possibilities.

'Not that I want to get married,' Rosalie continued. By now both Carole and Jude were convinced she was drunk – maybe she'd topped her level up beforehand to steel herself for the encounter with her ex. 'From what I've seen of my parents' marriage, there's no way I want to go down that route. I can be quite unhappy enough on my own without deliberately adding to the misery. It's easy enough to hate yourself. Marriage just spreads more hatred around, so that you end up hating everyone involved.'

'But when we talked,' said Carole reasonably, 'you implied that you loved your father.'

'Oh, I did. When I was twelve I adored him. And I thought he adored me too. But he seemed quite happy for me suddenly not to be part of his life. Just like that – one day I'm living with him, next I'm not. End of story. End of relationship. End of everything.'

'I thought you still saw him sometimes.'

'Been a while. My father, the ever-loving Hudson Vale, has got a new wife now. And twin daughters. Couldn't show any love to one daughter, but now he's lavishing it on two of the little buggers. Ridiculous for a man of his age to be going back to nappies and nursery school, isn't it? But that's what he's chosen.

'Maybe that's what all men are looking for – the secret of eternal youth. Shacking up with a younger woman is supposed to do the trick – certainly Kent kept saying how young I made him feel. The blood of young virgins – huh. And this lot—' her wide, unsteady gesture took in everyone present at the Fethering Yacht Club – 'are all trying to recapture a time when they were younger and less stressed, just "messing about in boats" . . .' She nodded derisively towards Quintus Braithwaite. 'Getting up to stupid things in their dinghies, playing secret games and—'

'What do you mean by that?' asked Carole eagerly. 'Do you actually know something that Quintus—?'

But Rosalie had already moved on. She swilled down the remains of her drink. 'So what shall I do now – make a scene? Really bugger up Kent and Sara's celebration. Tell Sara what a devious bastard she's taking on; spill the beans about all the shady deals he's been involved in over the years; destroy any hopes of happiness they might have?'

For a moment she looked as if she was about to put that plan into action. Then her shoulders slumped, tears started in her eyes and, with a mumbled, 'I must go', she edged her way through the crowd to the exit door.

'Do you think we should go after her?' asked Carole.

To her surprise, Jude shook her head. 'I think it's something she's got to sort out on her own.'

They might have had further discussion, had Sara Courtney not come across at that point to give them both lavish hugs. She too had had a little too much to drink, but it hadn't had the destructive effect on her that it had had on Rosalie Achter. Sara seemed positively to sparkle from head to toe. 'I'm having such a wonderful time,' she said. 'I'd given up hopes of ever having an engagement party.'

'Didn't I tell you you should, "Hang on in there"?'

'You did, Jude, you did. And bless you for it.' Sara let out a little giggle. 'Well, maybe you should be next.'

'Next to do what?' asked Carole.

'Get engaged. Get married – now it's legal for you.'

The look on Carole's face when she heard this was one that Jude would cherish for a long, long time.

TWENTY-FOUR

'Well, there's one positive thing we have got out of the evening,' said Jude.

They were sitting in the unkempt cosiness of Woodside Cottage's sitting room. The fire had just been lit and was beginning to draw. Though they had both had quite a lot at the Yacht Club, Jude had insisted they needed 'another drink to debrief'. And Carole hadn't put up much of an argument against the idea.

'What do you mean?' she asked.

'Related to the investigation.'

'Ah, you were thinking of what Rosalie said about Quintus Braithwaite getting up to secret things in dinghies.'

'I wasn't, actually, though I agree that might be something worth investigating.'

'Yes. And what's more, Jude, we've never really followed up on the theft of Quintus's dinghy, have we? You know, the night Sara saw the body.'

'You're right, and we will try to find out more about that, but the piece of information I was pleased we got this evening was the name of Rosalie's father.'

'Hudson Vale.'

'Exactly.'

'Well, apart from being a rather unusual name, in what other way is it of use to us?'

'It gives us an opportunity to find out more about Josie Achter.'

Carole still couldn't see where all this was leading. Jude explained, 'I've still got a feeling that there is some connection between the dead man and Josie Achter.'

'And where do you get that from? The corpse's *aura*?'

Jude was used to these jibes at her practices and beliefs, but as ever she didn't rise to this one, saying instead, 'I've just a feeling there's something relevant in the Achter family background – or perhaps I should say the Vale family background.'

'Well, if you say so.' Carole didn't sound convinced.

Jude produced her laptop and switched it on. 'Hudson Vale, Hudson Vale . . . there can't be many Hudson Vales around, can there?' She clicked through to Google and consulted the screen. 'Plenty about the Hudson Valley in New York State. And there's a road in Coventry actually called Hudson Vale.'

'I wish I knew what you were trying to find out,' said Carole plaintively.

'I'm just trying to get a contact for him. Ah, this looks promising.' She moved the laptop round so that Carole could see the screen. The website was headed: 'HUDSON VALE PHOTOGRAPHY'. And the examples of his work showed that he was more than just a wedding snapper.

There were pictures of supermodels and pop stars, portraits of minor royals and magazine spreads. When it came to photography, Hudson Vale was clearly near the top of the tree.

Jude clicked on to the 'Contact' page. There was an email address and a telephone number. If she'd had less to drink at the yacht club, she probably wouldn't have rung it at after nine in the evening. But as it was, she did.

The answering voice was gentle, public school educated. 'Hello?'

'Is that Hudson Vale?'

'Speaking.'

'I want to talk to you about your daughter Rosalie.'

'Oh God,' said the voice. 'You're not from the police again, are you?'

Hudson Vale didn't mind seeing them on a Saturday. 'Ergh,' he'd said on the phone, 'when I started in this business I had a wedding every bloody Saturday. At least thank God I don't have to do that any more. With brides you very quickly get simpered out.'

Their appointment was for eleven o'clock. As Carole's Renault joined the A3 at Milford, a cold, wintry rain began. It hadn't let up when she turned off the motorway, following the signs to Esher and Kingston, and looked as if it was set in for the day.

Hudson Vale was still living in the fine, five-bedroomed Georgian house he'd shared with Josie and Rosalie. He answered their knock on the door very promptly, as if he had been waiting in the hall for them. A tall, willowy man with long white hair and fashionably round, black-framed glasses over startlingly blue eyes, he led them through the house to his studio. Through a closed door they passed they could hear the sounds of his twin daughters playing, presumably with their mother, but Hudson made no reference to them.

The studio had been built on to the back of the house and to a very high spec. Presumably, if this was where he met his clients, it needed to be smart. Jude got the impression that it was a part of the house the two little girls were not allowed to enter.

What was striking was that, while the walls of the rooms they had come through had been decorated by paintings from various hands, in the studio everything on display was Hudson Vale's own work. Even more striking was how many of the photographs were of Rosalie; some in colour but most in monochrome. Black and white was clearly his favoured medium. Rosalie as a baby, Rosalie as a little girl, Rosalie trembling on the edge of adolescence. There was a particularly charming colour print of her, aged perhaps eleven, giving her father a big cuddle. The pale blond hair of the younger Hudson Vale contrasted with Rosalie's tight, jet-black curls, and his blue eyes sparkled with happiness.

There were no images of Rosalie after the age of eleven. To Jude the lavish display contrasted sharply with the complete lack of family photographs in Rosalie Achter's soulless flat in Fethering.

Hudson's studio was well equipped. Gesturing to the inevitable Italian machine, he offered his guests coffee. Jude asked for a cappuccino. Carole, who in a café would have demanded 'ordinary black coffee', asked for an Americano without milk.

The garden-facing wall of the studio was all glass doors, which could clearly concertina back to the sides when the weather was more clement. Though the rain was still lashing down and it was February, the garden was well tended and must have looked glorious in the summer. Jude commented on this while Hudson made the coffee.

'Yes, it's beautiful,' he responded. 'I have to confess I do rather love this office. Sometimes I almost resent having to leave it to go out and take photographs.' He gestured towards two closed doors. 'I'm very self-sufficient here, you see. Bathroom through there. The other's my darkroom.'

'I didn't know photographers still used darkrooms,' Carole observed.

'A lot of them don't. But I'm afraid I'm a bit of a Luddite when it comes to digital cameras. I prefer old-fashioned rolls of film. For me a lot of the most creative work happens in the processing. I can achieve a subtlety of tone then that I just can't get with the digital equipment.'

Carole looked round at the photos on display. 'Well, the effect is certainly wonderful.'

Jude too looked around. 'I can't help noticing—'

He was ahead of her. 'Yes, they all are of Rosalie. She has an amazingly expressive face.'

'But I gather you don't see much of her these days,' said Carole rather clumsily. Jude would have been more subtle.

Hudson Vale shrugged. 'No, I'm afraid I don't. I tried to see as much of her as possible after the divorce, but Josie didn't make it easy for me. Then, as she got into her teens, Rosalie seemed to turn against me, didn't want to see me. Which I suppose was fair enough. I'd been painted as "the man who done her mother wrong", so why should she want to spend time with me?'

'You're saying that's how Josie painted you?' asked Jude.

'Probably. Maybe not. It doesn't really matter what the reason was. Rosalie ceased to want to see me.' The memory was still painful to him. 'Then she went to college in Brighton and got in with a bad lot, and then I would only hear if she got in trouble with the police. Which was why I asked if you were the police last night. I had a horrible vision of the whole thing starting up again.'

'If you were estranged from Rosalie, why did the police get in touch with you rather than Josie?'

'Usually they'd tried Josie first. And she'd given them my number, saying our daughter was as much my responsibility as hers.'

There was a silence. 'What kind of trouble did Rosalie get into in Brighton?' asked Jude gently.

'Oh, mixing with the wrong set, drugs, you know. She actually had some boyfriends who were dealers, got very close to the gangs who were running the operation there. She mixed with some pretty nasty people, the kind who got involved with gunfights and . . .' He sighed. 'I know, she was the classic example of the nicely brought-up middle-class girl reacting against her nice middle-class upbringing. And in her case it was probably worse because of the divorce. I think a lot of her behaviour was just punishing me and her mother for having got divorced, having broken up the happy family . . . though I think she knew long before that that it wasn't really a happy family.'

'We saw Rosalie yesterday evening,' Jude announced suddenly.

'Oh, how was she?' The question was instinctively solicitous. However little he had seen of his daughter in recent years, there was no doubt that Hudson Vale still loved her.

'Well . . .' Carole looked across to Jude, checking how much information she should give. Granted permission, she said, 'It was actually at a party. She was pretty drunk.'

Hudson looked puzzled. 'I'm sorry to sound rude, but I can't quite imagine why you two would have been at the same kind of party as Rosalie.'

'I take your point. It was an engagement party for someone she worked with at Polly's Cake Shop.'

'That would make sense.'

'But,' said Jude deliberately, 'the man her friend was getting engaged to was a former lover of Rosalie's.'

'Ah.' He made no further comment.

'An older man,' Jude continued.

Hudson Vale shrugged. He had clearly given up trying to keep tabs on his estranged daughter's love life.

'I gather you've remarried,' said Carole, again more direct than Jude would have been.

'Yes. It's wonderful to be given a second chance in life.' But he didn't sound totally convinced by his own words.

'And has Rosalie met her half-sisters?'

He shook his head firmly. 'No. They belong to different chapters of my life.' Echoing the words of Janice Green. For a moment Carole wondered whether her own life was divided into chapters. And she came to the conclusion that it was. Childhood, the Home Office, David, Stephen, divorce, post-divorce, Fethering. And she wasn't really expecting any further chapters beyond Fethering. Yes, it was a way of looking at one's life, no worse and no better than any other.

Maybe Hudson's talk of 'chapters' had also reminded Jude of Janice Green, because her next question was: 'Does the name Amos Green mean anything to you?'

He shook his head. 'No. And it's a fairly unusual name, so I'd probably remember if I had heard it.'

'You might have seen something in the news about him,' said Carole. 'His body was found on Fethering Beach back in October.'

'Doesn't ring a bell. Why are you interested in him?'

'We actually had the misfortune to find his body on the beach,' said Jude. 'And we are pretty sure that he was murdered.'

'I see,' said Hudson. 'So, in answer to my question of last night, you are not the official police but a pair of intrepid amateur sleuths.'

Carole and Jude looked at each other rather shiftily. It was an accusation neither of them could deny.

'Look,' he went on, 'I agreed to see you this morning because I thought you might have some news of Rosalie. I'm not sure that I was planning to get involved in a murder investigation.'

'We fully understand that,' said Jude, 'but we're desperately trying to find some connection between Amos Green and Fethering.'

'Then I'm not quite sure why you're asking me. I haven't been to Fethering for years. And recently the only conversations I've had with Josie have been rather tight-lipped affairs over financial issues that didn't get properly sorted out in the divorce.'

'Do you mind if we ask you about the divorce?' asked Carole.

'Well, I can't really see what business it is of yours . . .'

'It isn't any of our business,' said Jude in a manner which was on the edge of flirtatious, 'but . . .'

It worked. He relented. Spreading his arms wide in a gesture of submission, he said, 'All right, ask me about the divorce. It's so long ago now that I'm not about to start weeping at the recollection.'

'Josie described your divorce to me as "sticky".'

'Show me the divorce that isn't sticky. When two people have invested a large chunk of their lives into something which turns out to be a complete disaster . . . well, it's not exactly a recipe for ecstasy, is it?'

There was a heartfelt 'No' from Carole, as Jude went on, 'Josie also said she got a very bad financial deal from you and your lawyer.'

'I'm sure she didn't just say "lawyer".'

'No. "Bastard lawyer" was her exact expression.'

'And no doubt "bastard ex-husband" came into the conversation as well.' Jude could not deny it. 'And no doubt she also complained about her having to live in a poky little flat in

Fethering, while I . . .' His gesture around the lavish studio meant
he didn't need any more words.

'Yes, I did get a bit of that too.'

'And presumably you also got lots of detail about my "unreasonable behaviour" being the reason for the divorce?'

'She did use those words, yes.'

'That would figure. Strange how, over the years, people create
their own versions of history. I'm sure Josie's narrative of the divorce
is very imaginative.'

'Well . . .'

'I never wanted a divorce. I'm not suggesting my relationship
with Josie was particularly good, but we managed to rub along. My
only reason for wanting to stay together was Rosalie. I was afraid
a split would do her irreparable damage . . .' He shook his head
gloomily. 'And it seems that I was right.'

'So it was Josie who asked for the divorce?'

'Yes.'

'But you say the marriage had jogged along all right for over ten
years. What was it that suddenly made her want to end it?'

'She'd met someone else. Or rather re-met someone else. She
never gave me any name for him, but she insisted this was the
real thing and she had to take her only possible chance of
happiness.'

'Did she say where she'd met him?' asked Carole.

'Not where she'd met him originally, no. But when he came back
into her life, it was at some yacht club on the south coast where a
friend of hers was having a fiftieth birthday bash. It was a Saturday
night, twelve, thirteen years ago. I wasn't there, off on some assign-
ment abroad, can't remember where.'

'This yacht club wouldn't have been in Fethering, would it?'

'Could have been.' Hudson Vale shook his long white hair. 'I
honestly can't remember. I was in a pretty emotional state at the
time – and very busy with my work. Career just taking off in a big
way – I'd got my first major magazine contract which was going
to involve lots of foreign travel – so I was kind of preoccupied.'

'And was that why Josie got custody of Rosalie in the divorce
settlement? Because you'd be travelling so much?'

'Yes, and the thinking was that I'd still see lots of her; you know,
there was a very civilized timetable arranged for my having access

to Rosalie, but Josie managed to screw that up – and to poison Rosalie's mind against me.'

'One thing that seems odd,' said Jude, 'is that, as far as we can tell, since she came to Fethering and opened Polly's Cake Shop, Josie's been on her own.'

'I really wouldn't know about that. I closed my mind to it.'

'So you'd have no idea what happened to the man for whom your wife left you?'

'None at all. On the occasions when I went to the Fethering flat to pick Rosalie up for my access days, I never saw any evidence of a man living there.'

'And you don't know any more about the man who Josie thought was "the real thing"?'

'Nope. As I said, I didn't want to find out about him. All I know was that he was married and that he travelled a lot.' He looked at his watch. He had been very co-operative so far, but maybe his patience was wearing a bit thin. 'I'm going to have to chuck you out soon,' he said. 'I promised my girls that I'd play with them. I tend to be very busy all week, so at weekends . . .'

'Yes, of course,' said Jude. 'We very much appreciate your having given up your time for us.'

'No problem. And if you see Rosalie . . .'

'Yes?'

'Give her my love, won't you?'

'Of course.'

'One thing . . .' said Carole.

'Mm?'

'Would you by any chance have a contact number for Josie's friend, the one whose fiftieth she attended?'

'I might well,' said Hudson Vale, switching on his tablet. 'I did the photographs for her wedding way back and I always keep all my clients' contact details. Yes, here it is – Becky Granger.' He read out the digits. 'That was her mobile. Whether she's still kept the same number, I've no idea.'

'Well, thank you, anyway.'

Hudson Vale rose from his chair and gestured towards the door. Carole and Jude also stood up. 'Just one more thing . . .' asked Jude.

'Yes? This is getting horribly *Columbo*, you know.' His tone was sharper. It was time they should be on their way.

'When I talked to Josie, she seemed very bitter.'

'I think that's not uncommon with divorcées.'

'But she was particularly bitter about anti-Semitism.'

'What?' Clearly that was the last thing Hudson Vale had been expecting.

'She said she'd experienced prejudice all her life and it was at its worst in "nice middle-class areas" like Fethering . . . or possibly Esher . . .'

'Well, I don't know where she got that from. It's certainly something I'd never been aware of during our marriage . . . and Josie never mentioned to me that she felt like that.'

'She also suggested that anti-Semitism was one of the causes of your breaking up.'

He looked genuinely amazed. 'I've no idea where she got that from. Right from the start, when I first met her I thought her being Jewish was wonderfully exotic. I felt so boringly blond and British. In fact, Josie's Jewishness was a big part of her attraction to me.'

TWENTY-FIVE

I n the Renault on the A3, Carole looked disapproving as she heard her neighbour blithely lying in her conversation to Becky Granger. 'I know it's ages ago, but I was at your fiftieth . . .'

'Not that many ages ago,' Becky Granger reproved her mildly from the other end of the phone. 'I'm not quite ready for the scrapheap yet.'

'Sorry. I was there with a boyfriend. You and I hadn't met before.'

'And I probably didn't meet you then. There were a lot of people there I didn't know. My then boyfriend was a member of the Fethering Yacht Club and I think he issued invitations to every other member. Extravagant bastard . . . one of the many reasons why we're no longer an item.' She sighed. 'Oh, it all seems a long time ago. That party was such a scrum.'

'Anyway, Becky, I got your number through Josie Achter.'

'Oh my God, I haven't heard that name for ages. How is the old boot? Still in Fethering? Still got the café?'

'No, she's sold up and moved to Hove.'

'Has she? I haven't heard a squeak from her for ages – probably not since that party.'

'And it was at the Fethering Yacht Club, wasn't it?'

'Blimey, how much did you have to drink that night? Yes, of course it was.'

Carole's lips were tight. To be able to hear Jude's blatant lies and not to be able to hear the other end of the conversation was doubly frustrating for her.

'Well, Becky, Josie and I were trying to remember the name of someone she met that night, someone she hadn't seen for a long time . . .?'

'Are we talking about the guy she spent the whole of the evening dancing with? They were all over each other. Which was so unlike Josie. Normally at parties she was all buttoned up, never wanted to draw attention to herself. But that evening . . . I'd have been embarrassed if I hadn't been in such a state that I was incapable of embarrassment.'

'It probably would be that guy she was talking about. Josie was saying she'd lost touch with him.'

'Well, she'd certainly found touch with him at the party.'

'So what was his name?'

'Oh my God, you're really testing me now. We are talking over ten years ago.'

'Please try and remember.'

'I am trying. Oh, it was one of those unusual man's names. Sounding old-fashioned. Ending with "us".'

'Amos?' asked Jude excitedly.

'No, not Amos. It was . . .' There was a silence. 'Quintus! That's right. His name was Quintus.'

TWENTY-SIX

'**G**ood God!' The Renault almost swerved dangerously when Carole had the conversation reported back to her. 'Josie Achter and Quintus Braithwaite! I can't believe it.'

'It does sound unlikely, I agree. But she had no reason to make it up. And it fits the minimal description Hudson gave us. "Married and travelled a lot." Quintus Braithwaite had many foreign postings and was often away at sea.'

'Yes, but . . . to think of him as the great love of Josie Achter's life, the reason why she got divorced . . . it doesn't sit very comfortably with me.'

'Nor me. But it must be true. There's also the fact that Quintus Braithwaite's dinghy was stolen and used on the night of October the third.'

'Are you suggesting he took it himself?'

'Yes.'

'What, to dispose of Amos Green's body?'

'I suppose so.' Jude felt confused. 'I don't know.'

'But his affair with Josie – if such a thing ever happened – must have been over long ago. Quintus Braithwaite is a pompous bore and an idiot, but I really can't see him as a murderer.'

'It's always the unlikely ones . . .' Jude suggested.

A disgruntled 'Huh' was heard from Carole. 'I'm sure we're barking up a tree that's so wrong it's not even in the right country. I thought we set out today trying to find something that connected the late Amos Green with Fethering. And have we got anything?'

Jude was forced to concede that they hadn't. 'The only tenuous link we do have is that Binnie Swales served him in Polly's on the afternoon of the third of October.'

Carole nodded. 'Yes.' Then a recollection came to her. 'Do you remember when we went to the Crown and Anchor after the relaunch of Polly's Community Café?'

'Yes.'

'Binnie said then that she used to serve behind the bar at Fethering Yacht Club.'

Jude caught the excitement in her friend's voice. 'And you're thinking she might have been on duty on the night of Becky Granger's fiftieth? That she might have seen Josie and Quintus dancing together?'

'Well, it's worth asking, isn't it?'

Binnie's house was one of the few fishermen's cottages in Fethering not to have undergone gentrification. Most of them were now owned by rich weekenders from London who – while keeping the lines of the quaint eighteenth-century exteriors – had refurbished everything inside to the highest possible spec.

But, though ungentrified, Binnie's had not been left in its pristine pre-war state. There was a row of these cottages on the opposite side of the Fether estuary from the yacht club. Right next door to Kent Warboys' conversion. Originally the sheds from which his home had been created had served the owners of the cottages as storage space, workshops and a small factory in which their wives gutted and prepared the day's catch for sale.

The back of the cottages had a fine view over the English Channel, much appreciated by their twenty-first-century owners (though the first owners probably never looked that way, being already sick to the back teeth of the sea).

The outside of Binnie's cottage might have looked shabby and run down, but the interior had been extensively redecorated. Redecorated, however, very much in Binnie's style, reflecting the range of colours in the clothes she wore.

In spite of the smallness of her hall, its space was dominated by a stuffed badger. Astride it like a miniature jockey was a purple teddy bear. The walls were papered in diagonal stripes of silver and gold. The front parlour into which Carole and Jude were ushered was equally eccentric. And if the sitting room at Woodside Cottage could be described as 'cluttered', a new word would have to be coined for Binnie's.

It was just the sheer range of objects in the room that took one's breath away. Every surface was covered with an eclectic collection which included carved wooden miniature chairs, ceramic figurines, glass bon-bons, Indian jewellery, ivory elephants and a stuffed owl.

The walls were thick with movie posters, chalk drawings, metal advertising signs for Bird's Custard and 'Virol – for Anaemic Girls', royal souvenir mugs and sepia photographs of World War One Tommies. To accommodate yet more stuff, wires had been fixed across the ceiling, and from these hung parasols, bouquets of artificial flowers, plastic medals on ribbons, a policeman's helmet, some brass cooking utensils, wooden tennis rackets and a rubber vampire bat.

Binnie was dressed that Saturday in a kind of orange string vest over a scarlet twinset, an electric blue PVC miniskirt, horizontally striped tights in green and yellow and silver ballet shoes. She noticed them looking round as they entered the front parlour. 'And every single thing in this room has a story attached to it. Some people write autobiographies . . .' She gestured to the confusion of objects around her. 'This is my autobiography. A story behind everything here.'

'I'm sure it's all fascinating,' said Carole, aware that her words were coming out more harshly than she intended, 'but actually it's not that we want to talk to you about.'

Binnie Swales did not look too upset by the rejection of her life story. 'Fine. Would you like some tea or coffee?' She chuckled. 'I've had a little experience of serving tea and coffee.'

'No, we're fine,' said Jude, answering for both of them. 'Just had coffee.' It wasn't true but they didn't want anything to delay the progress of their investigation.

'What we really want you to do,' said Carole, 'is to cast your mind back to the days when you were working behind the bar at the Fethering Yacht Club . . .'

'Well, there were plenty of those. Any particular day you had in mind?'

'It was probably about twelve, thirteen years ago, a Saturday night. Might you have been working then?'

'Could have been.'

'It was a fiftieth birthday party,' said Jude.

'The yacht club bar's seen a good few of those.'

'I'm sure it has.'

'I mean, it hasn't got much in the way of facilities. Not a potential "wedding venue" like Chichester Yacht Club and some of the other big ones are. But if you want a local piss-up in Fethering, you're not exactly spoiled for choice, so you might as well get pissed in the yacht club.'

Jude tried to get back to the subject, saying, 'The woman whose birthday it was was called Becky Granger.'

Binnie shook her head. 'Name doesn't mean anything to me. Mind you, it's quite possible I helped out at the party and never heard her name. Bookings for that kind of thing went through the Vice-Commodore.'

'Do you have a name for him?' asked Carole eagerly.

'Yes. He was called Denis Woodville.' Carole and Jude exchanged looks. They remembered meeting him when they were investigating the death of Aaron Spalding. 'But I'm afraid you won't get anything out of him now. Died five or six years back.'

'Ah. Pity.'

'Well, possibly not that big a pity.' Clearly Binnie had not warmed to that particular Vice-Commodore. 'He was a pompous git, like they all are down the yacht club. Any other way you can single out this particular fiftieth?'

'I gather everyone got pretty drunk,' said Carole.

'I asked if you could "single it out". Everyone gets pretty drunk at every fiftieth birthday party.'

'Yes. Sorry.'

'Apparently Quintus Braithwaite was among the guests at this particular one.'

'Was he? That'd be quite unusual. Before he retired, he was off abroad so much that he didn't come to the yacht club that often.'

'He was definitely there that night. Apparently made quite a show of himself on the dance floor.'

'Oh God.' Binnie let out a raucous laugh. 'Now it comes back to me. Quintus Braithwaite – "Dad Dancing" at its most ghastly. Yes, he'd had a skinful that night.'

'Was his wife there?'

'The sainted Phoebe? She wasn't, actually. On holiday with the kids somewhere so far as I can recall. No, Quintus was on his own in Fethering. I couldn't imagine him behaving like he did if Phoebe had been around.'

'You talk about his "Dad Dancing",' said Jude, 'but who was he doing the dancing with?' She thought the question was a better approach than actually mentioning Josie Achter's name.

'Well, that was the really strange thing about it.'

'Oh?'

'He danced with the most unlikely person in the room. Woman who became my boss.'

'Josie Achter?' Carole couldn't stop herself from saying the name.

'Yes, you're right. If ever there was an unlikely coupling . . . I can only think that Josie had been at the booze as much as Quintus had. I'd always thought of her as uptight, even a bit prim – but that night . . . God, nobody was going to forget the way they saw them dance that night . . . virtually pushed everyone else off the floor.'

'And do you know,' asked Jude, 'whether she and Quintus left the yacht club together that night?'

'Sorry, I've no means of knowing. End of an evening like that, you're so knackered, all you want to do is get home to bed, but there are still all the glasses to be collected up and cleaned, the debris of the food to be cleared, crockery and cutlery to be put in the dishwasher. Then there's always a hardcore of the boozy lot who want to go on drinking all night, and all you want to do is get to bed and . . . In answer to your question, no. I have no idea who went home with who that night.'

'And do you know if the relationship developed?'

'Quintus and Josie? No idea. Seems unlikely.'

'But surely,' said Carole, 'in a place like this, there must've been a lot of gossip.'

'Oh, sure. Yes, for the week or so afterwards, nobody talked about anything else. Plenty of sniggering in the yacht club, for sure, and I'd just started doing the odd shift at Polly's, so I heard a lot of idle chatter there too. But then I think Quintus went off abroad again and it all died down.'

'And the pair of them have never been seen together since?'

'Well, I've certainly never seen them together since.'

'Not even in Polly's?'

'Quintus used to go there from time to time, more since he's been retired, but he'd always got Phoebe with him. And I suppose there may have been occasions that Josie was also in the café in a professional capacity when the Braithwaites came in for a coffee, but I never saw them behave to each other in any way that was unusual.'

'So,' asked Carole, 'what is the verdict of the Fethering grapevine on what happened between the two of them?'

'Both got very drunk one night and behaved in a way that was totally out of character for them.'

'End of story,' said Jude glumly.

'End of that story, so far as I can tell,' said Carole gloomily.

'And end of the Polly's Cake Shop story.' Binnie sighed. 'I can't believe how much I miss working there.'

'Would you really have wanted to go on with Phoebe Braithwaite as your manager?' asked Carole.

'No, the last month of working out my notice was a right pain from beginning to end. The lovely Phoebe had no interest in her staff . . . well, the members of staff who weren't stuck-up bitches like she is. And I could see the whole thing was falling apart, and her precious volunteers were leaving in droves, but there was no way she was going to take any advice from anyone. No help from anyone either.'

'Did you offer your services?'

'Of course. Every time one of her toffee-nosed volunteers failed to turn up for a shift I offered to step into the breach. And every time she said, "No, I'm sorry, Binnie. That wouldn't look right. You see, I am trying to update the image of Polly's".'

Jude let out a dry chuckle. 'I'm surprised you didn't punch her in the face.'

'Oh, I've been insulted by better women than Phoebe Braithwaite. No skin off my nose. But then when it was actually my last day, the volunteers were in a worse state than usual – they'd all volunteered to go off and do other things, like go skiing or "take Gabriel to the Pony Club". And I said to her, "Look, Phoebe, I know today's the last day I'm being paid for, but I am prepared to come back, anytime you want, as a volunteer."'

'That was very generous of you.'

'Well, I loved the place, didn't I? I didn't enjoy seeing it going downhill.'

'And what was Phoebe's reaction?' asked Carole.

'Oh, same old, same old. "That's most kind of you, dear Binnie, but I'm afraid that wouldn't work, you know, you being here as a volunteer. I'm afraid you wouldn't fit in with Polly's new image." Well, stuff that, I thought, and I haven't been back there since. Which is just as well, because I gather the place has now closed down for good.'

'We're not absolutely sure that's going to happen,' said Jude. 'The Action Committee still have hopes of reopening it with a new management structure.'

'I won't hold my breath,' said Binnie.

'But if it were to reopen . . .' Carole began tentatively, 'under a professional manager . . . and with a different sort of volunteers . . . and you were asked to help out . . .?'

Jude was pleased to hear Carole's words. They meant that she hadn't rejected out of hand the possibility of managing the Volunteer Rota in a revamped Polly's.

'Who knows?' was Binnie's reply. 'I've seen too many local Community Projects fall apart to get overexcited about the chances of Polly's rising from the grave.'

'Well, I hope you're wrong,' said Jude.

'Oh, so do I. Nothing I'd like more than being back waitressing there . . . under any regime. That is, any regime but one. I'd be quite happy if Hitler or Stalin was in charge, but there's no way I'm ever again going to work under Phoebe Braithwaite.'

Jude chuckled. 'You'll be all right on that score. The Braithwaites are completely out of the equation now. They have adjourned to focus their considerable energies on messing up some other charity.'

'I'm very glad to hear it.'

'So if the café does reopen,' Carole persisted, 'you might consider working there for free?'

'Oh yes. If it happens. It's not the money, you see. I can manage all right on my pension. And . . .' she waved around at her personal museum '. . . none of this paraphernalia is expensive. I just buy stuff I like. No, it's the people I miss at Polly's. I'd happily work there for free.'

'Well, we'll see what can be done,' said Jude.

The old woman shook her head. 'I'm not optimistic.'

'Going back to another matter, Binnie . . .'

'Yes, Carole?'

'This is a long shot, but presumably from the back of this house you get a very good view of the sea?'

'Yes, I like it. One of the reasons why we bought the place.'

'We?'

'Yes. I was married when I came to Fethering.'

'Oh? And . . .?' Carole put the enquiry as delicately as she could.

'My husband died within two years of our arriving here. Pancreatic cancer. Three weeks from diagnosis to death.'

'I'm frightfully sorry.'

'Don't worry, Carole. It's been a while.'

Jude observed that Binnie didn't wear a wedding ring.

'No, I took it off after he died. To my mind a marriage involves two people. Take one away, it's no longer a marriage. Also, wearing a wedding ring can inhibit other possibilities in one's life. I didn't want to announce to the world that I was *hors de combat* so far as sex was concerned.'

'And did the plan work?' asked Jude, with the smallest twinkle in her eye.

Binnie's eyes twinkled back as she said, 'I had my moments. Not love, obviously. My husband was the only one I was ever going to love, but . . . I had my moments.' She looked puzzled for a moment. 'How did we get on to that?'

'I was asking about the view from the back of your house.'

'Oh yes, that's right, Carole. Yes, I love it. My bedroom faces out the back. I don't sleep too well these days and I like nothing better than looking out over the night-time sea, watching the lights of the ships as they cross to and fro. Making up stories for them, where they've come from, where they're going to, that kind of thing. And of course in the daytime I enjoy watching the little boats too. I know who a lot of them belong to, you know, from my time at the Fethering Yacht Club. There are some very good sailors round here. Some very bad ones too. Weekenders from London who buy the biggest boats they can to show how much money they've got while they haven't got the first idea of how to actually sail the things. Quite funny sometimes. From my bedroom I see them leaving the yacht club moorings and then getting swept out by the current of the Fether. Haven't a clue what they're doing. More often than not, their first few trips end up with calls to the coastguard for someone to come out and tow them back in. Then they don't come down to the Fethering Yacht Club so often. Take up golf at Goodwood instead, perhaps. You'd be surprised how many of those big boats moored at the Fethering Yacht Club don't get taken out to sea from one year's end to the next. Their owners are actually afraid to use them.'

'I was just thinking,' said Jude, 'back to October the third, you know, the Saturday when you served Amos Green in Polly's Cake Shop . . .?'

'Yes, I wondered when you were going to get on to that.'

'Well, I was wondering, that evening after work, when you came back here, did you watch the sea out of your bedroom window?'

'Course I did. I do that every night. Much more interesting than anything I've ever seen on the telly. That's why I don't have a telly.'

'But you can only see during daylight?' asked Carole. 'Presumably once it gets dark, you can't see anything other than the lights?'

'You can see most of what goes on inshore and, you know, round the estuary. There's quite a lot of light spillage from the streetlamps along the Parade. They don't get turned off until eleven.'

'But that particular evening,' Jude went on, 'did you see anything strange?'

'What kind of strange?'

'Anyone out there in a small boat . . .' Jude hazarded, 'you know, a dinghy, probably rowing it?'

Binnie grinned complacently. 'Yes, I did see someone.'

'Do you know who it was?'

She shook her head. 'Too dark to see that.'

'Or how many people were in the boat?'

Another shake of the head.

'But did you recognize the actual boat?'

'Oh yes. I know who owns all the boats in Fethering.'

Jude couldn't wait. 'And was it,' she asked, 'the blue-painted rowing boat that belongs to Quintus Braithwaite?'

'Oh no,' replied Binnie. 'It came from much closer than that.'

'What do you mean?'

'It was an inflatable. A silver rubber dinghy. The one Kent Warboys keeps at the end of his garden.'

TWENTY-SEVEN

Both Carole and Jude looked flabbergasted. 'So what do you reckon they were doing in the boat?' asked Jude breathlessly.

'Well, as I say, I couldn't see.' Binnie Swales was clearly enjoying her moment in the spotlight. 'But, piecing it together, working from the available information . . .' Was she actually sending up their roles as amateur sleuths? '. . . one might conclude that the boat was being used to dispose of the body of Amos Green.'

'Why do you say that? How do you know he was dead?'

'You two found his dead body on the beach, didn't you? He was certainly dead then.'

'Yes, but that was about three weeks later. How did you know he was dead on the evening of the third of October?'

'Well, I'd seen him dead, hadn't I?'

'You mean you saw him being killed?'

'No, Carole, I didn't say that, did I? Listen to what I say. I said I saw him dead.'

'Yes.'

'Which means just that. I saw him dead.'

'Earlier that evening?' asked Jude.

'Yes.'

'Did you see him in the store room at Polly's?'

Binnie nodded. 'It was after closing time. I'd said goodbye to Sara, who was the only other member of staff still there. Hammo and the rest had gone home. Then Sara went to take some rubbish out to the recycling bins at the back and I suddenly remembered we were nearly out of doilies for the cake stands. So I thought I'd just check we'd got some in the store room and, if we hadn't, I'd write them down on the "To Buy" list in the kitchen.

'So I went into the store room.' She was silent, pacing her narrative.

'And?' demanded Carole.

'And I saw the body of the man who I'd served with an Americano that afternoon.'

'He was dead?'

'Definitely. There was a hole in his temple. Very little blood.'

'Any sign of a gun?' asked Jude.

'One on the window sill. And no, there was no way he could have shot himself there and then fallen across the room. He was too far away from the gun. Someone else shot him, that's for definite.'

There was a long, bewildered silence at the end of this narrative.

Then Carole said, 'Binnie, have you told anyone else about what you saw?'

'No.'

'Why not?'

'Nobody asked.'

TWENTY-EIGHT

T hey didn't get much more out of Binnie. Not that she was unwilling to speak, she just didn't have much more to tell them. She had seen the body in the store room, closed the door and gone home. She had never even contemplated informing the police. 'I thought somebody else'd find the body soon enough, no point in me getting myself involved. And I do remember from the days when I used to watch crime series on the telly that the person who discovers the body is always the first suspect, and I could do without all that hassle of questioning and what-have-you.'

'But didn't you find it odd,' Carole had asked, 'when there was nothing in the media about the body being found in Polly's?'

Binnie had shrugged. 'Yes. But it wasn't my business.'

'And thinking of who might have killed Amos Green – did you reckon that was your business?'

'Some things it's best not to get involved in.'

'So . . .' Jude had asked, 'you really haven't any suspicions at all as to who might be the murderer?'

'Not really, no.'

'What does that mean?'

'Just that the last thing the dead man did, you know, when I gave him the bill for his coffee, was to ask if Josie Achter was around.'

'And you told him that she was in Brighton for the day.'

'Yes, because that's what I'd been told. But presumably she came back from Brighton at some stage.'

In a way they had both known that there would come a moment when the investigation was bound to point towards Josie Achter. Like roads and Rome, everything seemed to lead back to her.

They had no contact number. She was still either in her hotel in Hove or, if the sale had gone through, in her new flat. Carole and Jude had no idea what either of those addresses were. And Rosalie had very firmly told Jude that her mother didn't want her new mobile number given out.

They racked their brains for ways to get in touch with her. Since Josie had mentioned being a part of the Jewish community in Hove, Carole wondered whether they should try contacting the synagogue there. Surely they'd have contact lists for their congregation?

Then Jude remembered something that had been said at the EGM when Kent Warboys announced that he was the owner of Polly's Cake Shop.

'What, you think he'd have a number for Josie Achter?'

'I should think he probably would.'

'Well, we're going to have to contact him at some point.' Carole grimaced. 'To ask him about the use of his rubber dinghy on the night Amos Green's body disappeared.'

'Yes, but I don't want to do that yet. Not until we've got more information about that evening.'

'Very well, but why are you—'

'At that EGM, Kent said the SPCS Action Committee Treasurer had sat in on a couple of his meetings with Josie Achter.'

'And you're thinking he might have a mobile number for her?'

'Exactly.'

Jude had been right. When she rang Alec Walters he was quite happy to give her the number.

'Shall I ring her straight away?' asked Jude, uncharacteristically vacillating.

'Yes, definitely.'

There was no reply and no means of leaving a message.

'Maybe it's because it's the Sabbath,' said Carole. 'Try again in the morning.'

On the Sunday morning the phone was answered. When Jude identified herself, it was clear that Josie Achter had not been to charm school since their last encounter. 'I have nothing to say to you,' she said.

'I'm ringing in connection with the death of Amos Green.'

That did get a response – or at least stopped Josie from switching her phone off. 'What do you know about his death?'

'A friend and I have been doing some investigation.'

'Why?'

'Because we're intrigued by what happened. We don't think Amos Green committed suicide. We think he was murdered.'

'We'd better talk,' said Josie Achter.

She was still living in the hotel – she hadn't quite completed on her new flat – but she didn't want to talk in the lounge there or a place like a pub or café. Though the day before's rain had continued unremittingly, she led them down to an empty shelter on the sea front.

'So what's all this about?' she asked. She came across to Carole and Jude as both tentative and probing. She wasn't about to give them any information until she knew how much they knew.

'We have discovered,' said Jude, 'that the day he died, Amos Green was in Fethering.'

'So what's that to do with me?'

'He came into Polly's that afternoon looking for you.'

'How do you know that?'

'Binnie told us. She served him.'

'Right. You say "the day he died". When his body was washed up on Fethering Beach he had already been dead for some time. How do you know when he died?'

'His body was seen in the store room at Polly's late that afternoon. The third of October. There was a gun in the room as well, but too far away for him to have used it on himself.'

'Did either of you see the body?' Josie was still assessing the extent of their knowledge.

'No.'

'Then who did see it?'

'Sara Courtney told me she'd seen the body in the store room,' said Jude.

'But Binnie had seen it before she did,' said Carole.

'Hm.' The wind lashed against the thick glass of the shelter, wetting their shoes. It was bitterly cold.

'So,' Jude pressed on, 'you can't deny that there was some connection between you and Amos Green.'

'I'm not denying it. So has your assiduous amateur sleuthing worked out what that connection was?'

'We talked to your ex-husband yesterday,' said Carole.

'God, you have been thorough.'

'He said that your marriage broke up because you'd met someone else.'

'Did he?'

'Or rather, re-met someone else.'

'Yes, that's what happened.'

'And we know when and where you re-met him,' said Jude.

'Remind me.' Josie Achter still retained her carapace of cynicism, but she was clearly shaken by the amount of information they were producing.

'About twelve years ago. At Fethering Yacht Club. At a party to celebrate Becky Granger's fiftieth birthday.'

Her face registered that that was a big shock. 'How on earth do you know this stuff?'

'Hudson was very helpful to us.'

'Yes, he bloody would be.'

'But things didn't quite work out, did they?' Carole observed. 'You got divorced because you'd re-met a former lover, but in the event the two of you didn't end up together. Had the idea been that he would get divorced too?'

'We'd talked about it.'

'But it seems he didn't keep his side of the bargain, did he? He went back to his wife . . . assuming his wife ever even knew that he had cheated on her.'

'His wife knew he had affairs,' said Josie in a matter-of-fact tone.

'Wasn't it difficult for you,' asked Carole, 'having them living so close to you?'

'Close?'

'You at Polly's Cake Shop, Quintus and Phoebe Braithwaite in the Shorelands Estate.'

Josie Achter looked at Carole in amazement, then burst into harsh laughter. 'You think the love of my life was Quintus Braithwaite? I'm not sure whether that's more funny or insulting. You imagine that I could even bear to touch that pompous oaf?'

'Well, apparently you were all over each other at Becky Granger's fiftieth.'

'That is just a measure of how effective my little plan was. I wanted people to talk about how Quintus and I behaved that night at the yacht club, but it never occurred to me they'd still be talking about it twelve years on.'

'What you're saying,' suggested Jude, 'is that dancing with Quintus all evening was just a smokescreen?'

'Exactly that. I loathe him – always have. But that evening I knew the ghastly Phoebe was out of the country. I also knew that he'd respond if I came on to him – he always had been a bit of a groper. What's more, he'd been at the booze all evening. It wasn't difficult.'

'And you needed the smokescreen,' said Jude with sudden insight, 'because Amos Green was also at the party and you didn't want people to suspect there was anything between you and him?'

'That was it,' Josie admitted. 'I couldn't believe my eyes when I saw Amos in the yacht club. He was having a thing with a friend of Becky's, not that that lasted once we were back together again. My feelings for him were as strong as ever. And he said he felt the same. And from that moment, I knew I couldn't continue the masquerade of my marriage to Hudson. I had to be with Amos; that was all there was to it.'

'Except of course he wasn't good "husband material", was he?' said Jude, quoting Janice Green.

'No. Mind you, I'm still glad I divorced Hudson. That wasn't going anywhere. Never had been.'

'But you must have been aware of the effect that divorce was going to have on Rosalie.'

'Not really. She was entering adolescence, not the best time of a girl's life. I don't know that our getting divorced made that much worse for her than it would have been anyway.' She spread her hands wide in a gesture of helplessness. 'You can't make an omelette without . . .'

Jude recoiled from the callousness in the woman's voice. Carole asked, 'So you and Amos Green never cohabited?'

'No. The affair continued until the divorce was final. Then he disappeared again. Never good at taking responsibility for his actions. When one of his women got serious it frightened him. As your friend said, not good "husband material".'.

'Well, at least he's not hurting any more women now.'

'No.' And to the surprise of both Carole and Jude, a tear glinted at the corner of Josie Achter's eye.

'So,' asked Jude, 'you didn't see him the day he died? That Saturday, the third of October?'

'No, I was spending the Shabbat – the Sabbath – with my widowed mother in Brighton. I didn't get back to Fethering till nearly eleven.'

'And you didn't look in the store room?'

'Why would I do that? At that time of night?'

'So you've no idea when the body was moved?'

'For God's sake! I didn't know there was a body there. The first I knew about Amos's death was when I saw a photograph of him on the television news.'

'And how did you react?'

'I was devastated. I had long since reconciled myself to the fact that we'd never be together, but I was amazed how much it hurt to know that I would never see him again.'

'And did you think he had committed suicide?'

'Never for a moment. Amos did not hate himself. He loved himself.'

'So who do you think killed him?' asked Jude.

'Assuming, that is, that you didn't?' Carole dared to add.

Josie Achter looked at her bleakly. 'You don't understand, do you? I loved Amos. He had hurt me more than anyone I knew, but that didn't stop me loving him.'

'So who do you think killed him?' Jude repeated.

'I've no idea,' Josie replied wearily.

'Where was Rosalie that day?' asked Carole.

'She was with me in Brighton.'

'Really?' Carole looked unconvinced. 'Sharing the Shabbat with your widowed mother? Rosalie told me she'd given up what she called "all that Jewish crap".'

'She was always very close to her grandmother. She bonded more with her than she ever did with me. For her grandmother, Rosalie would pretend that she still believed "all that Jewish crap".'

'But she didn't come back to Fethering with you that night?'

'Of course not.' Josie wrinkled her nose. 'She stayed in her squalid little flat in Brighton, surrounded by all her druggie friends.'

'What we haven't talked about . . .' said Jude gently, 'is the first time you met Amos Green.'

'No, we haven't,' Josie agreed shortly.

'How did you meet?'

'It was fairly soon after Hudson and I got married. We had just bought the house in Esher and he was using one of the spare bedrooms to work in. Which wasn't ideal because he couldn't really see clients there. So we had plans drawn up for a proper studio to be built on the back of the house.'

'We were in it yesterday morning,' said Carole.

'Oh, yes. Anyway, Hudson was very busy as ever, so we agreed that I'd sort of follow through the progress of the planning application, which involved a lot of trips to Kingston and . . .'

'And Amos Green was on the planning committee,' Carole completed the sentence for her.

'Yes. And we fell for each other just like that. It was a terribly difficult time for me. Because I realized what a massive mistake I had made in marrying Hudson. I had thought what I felt for him was as good as love got, and then when I met Amos . . . this sounds terribly corny, but I knew it was the real thing.'

'And you didn't consider just cutting your losses and moving in together?'

'Oh, we talked about it, yes. But we were both so recently married and we felt we had loyalties and . . . In retrospect we were very stupid. We should have followed our instincts, but . . . we didn't. And then life got complicated.'

'In what way?'

'Amos got into trouble in connection with the planning committee. There were allegations that he had been accepting bribes from some architects to give favourable responses to their planning applications.'

'Do you know if they were true?'

Josie shrugged. 'I didn't quite honestly care. All I knew at the time was that it meant I could see even less of Amos. Our time was tight enough, what with the demands of our spouses, and then Amos had to keep going off to give evidence at enquiries and . . . It was a very difficult time for both of us.

'And then I fell pregnant with Rosalie and that seemed to be a sign for me. A sign that we should end it. If we'd set up together, Amos would never have coped with the responsibility of bringing up a child. Hudson would clearly provide a much more stable background. He'd be a much better father for Rosalie.'

Jude looked steadily into the woman's dark eyes. 'Even if he wasn't actually her father?'

Josie Achter gave the words exactly the same emphasis as she repeated, 'Even if he wasn't actually her father.'

'Did Amos Green even know you were pregnant?' asked Carole.

Josie shook her head. 'He was under so much pressure at the time . . . I couldn't have added to it.'

'And do you know if he was ever prosecuted for taking bribes?'

'I don't know. I do know that he had to resign as a councillor.'

'Did he talk to you about the details of the case against him?'

'Not much. All he did say was that if he ever decided to take up blackmail he'd got a lot of information on a lot of architects' practices that could be extremely valuable one day.'

'Did he name any of those companies?' asked Jude.

'I'm sure he did, but it's a long time ago and it was at a pretty stressful time for me. Oh, actually I do remember one – and only because it was such a dreadful name. "Fit The Build".'

'Oh,' said Jude, remembering when Kent Warboys had told her the really bad name of one of his former companies.

TWENTY-NINE

Jude rang Kent from the Renault on the way back from Brighton. The rain had eased off but it was still a truculent-looking day. Dark clouds augured more bad weather to come.

Maybe Kent had been anticipating a call. He certainly seemed to recognize the seriousness of what they wanted to talk to him about. He was at home. Sara was out doing a major shop at Sainsbury's. Carole and Jude were welcome to drop by for 'a drink and a chat'.

As they approached the house, they were aware again of how close it was to the Fethering Yacht Club. The two buildings stood either side of the Fether estuary, both with large windows facing out to sea and smaller ones looking directly at each other.

Kent led them up to his magnificent sitting room and again made the offer of 'coffee or' – gesturing to a drinks cupboard – 'something stronger; it's certainly time for a Sunday lunchtime drink.' But both women refused. They wanted to get on with the conversation that was no longer avoidable.

'It goes back to the night of the third of October,' said Carole.

'And it also goes back a lot further,' Jude added. 'To the time when you had an architectural company in the Kingston area.'

'Ah yes. Rather a messy period of my professional life. And presumably it also goes back to any dealings I might have had with Amos Green?'

'Yes,' said Carole, in stern, avenging angel mode.

'Right.' He looked across towards the drinks cupboard. 'I'm going to get myself a drink. Are you sure you . . .?'

Both women shook their heads. Kent Warboys sighed and went to pour himself a large scotch. Then he turned to face them, his back to the picture window and the turbulent sea. 'I don't know how much you know already.'

'We know that you used to have a company called "Fit The Build" in the Kingston area,' said Carole.

He winced. 'I'll never get over what a terrible name it was.'

'And at that stage you had some dealings with Amos Green, who was on the planning committee.'

'And who subsequently had to resign from the planning committee,' Jude pointed out.

'Yes, okay. Well, it was the usual thing. Shabby, small-town corruption. Amos Green was found to have been guilty of taking bribes to ease through planning applications. We're not talking big sums of money here, just the occasional small incentive. Often it wasn't even money. Tickets for Wimbledon, major golf events, expensive meals out, cases of vintage wine delivered. Where is the point when backscratching becomes bribery?'

'And Fit The Build was involved in this?' asked Carole implacably.

'Yes, most of the companies round there were. It was a more relaxed time. You'd find the same sort of stuff going on in most local planning authorities. Fit The Build was wound up very soon after all this happened. I needed to start out again with a clean slate.'

'But,' asked Jude, 'did Amos Green have information about his dealings with Fit The Build that you would rather never came out into the open?'

'Well, I suppose there was some stuff that could have been harmful to the company's image at the time but, as I said, Fit The Build was very quickly wound up.'

Carole's eyes were still fixed on his face. 'So did Amos Green have information about the running of Fit The Build that could still cause you trouble if he spilled the beans?'

'I'm sure if he ever did want to make the information public, my lawyers could have sorted out some deal agreeable to both parties.'

'Paid him off, you mean?'

Kent Warboys shrugged. 'I don't like the expression, but yes, I'm sure something could have been sorted out.'

'But the question is,' said Jude, 'did Amos Green ever threaten to blackmail you?'

'Never.'

'He didn't approach you recently?'

'No.'

'Not at any time round the third of October last year?'

'Absolutely not. I haven't seen anything of Amos Green from the time he resigned from the Kingston planning committee. Hadn't thought about him, either, until I saw his photo on the television news and heard his body had been found here in Fethering.'

He sounded convincing, but then again, whatever his agenda, Kent Warboys was the kind of man who would always make himself sound convincing.

'Going back to that third of October weekend . . .' said Carole. 'Yes?'

She gestured towards the garden. 'Your boat down there, the rubber dinghy, was used on the evening of that Saturday.'

'Huh,' he said bitterly. 'You can't do anything unseen in a place like Fethering. Always some old biddy watching out.'

Neither Carole nor Jude chose to identify the 'old biddy' in question.

'There is not definite proof,' Carole went on, 'but it seems quite likely that your rubber dinghy was used to dispose of Amos Green's body at sea.'

Now their words were getting too close to accusation. 'I have no idea if that's what happened or not. She just asked if she could borrow the dinghy and I said yes. She didn't tell me what she wanted it for.'

'So you didn't help. You didn't row the boat out or—?'

'I didn't touch the dinghy that evening. I just gave her permission to use it. I knew she was in a terrible state emotionally, and when it's someone to whom you've been really close, well . . .'

There was a sound from downstairs of the front door opening and Sara's voice called out, 'Car's absolutely filled to the gunwales, Kent. Could you come and give me a hand unloading it?'

The architect put his finger to his lips. 'Don't mention anything we've talked about to Sara.'

'I think perhaps we should,' said Carole.

THIRTY

S ara still had the mobile number on her contacts list from the time when she had been working at Polly's Cake Shop. It was answered rather blearily on the fourth ring.

And without argument a meeting was agreed. Carole and Jude got back into the Renault and retraced their route eastwards along the A27.

The area certainly lived up to its 'manky' description. Brighton is famous for its splendid seafront, the Regency Pavilion and the trendy chaos of the Lanes; but there's another side to the town, a warren of dilapidated houses, whose boards of non-matching bell-pushes signify transient multi-occupancy.

Rosalie Achter was subdued as she let them in. It was a one-bedroom flat with a door leading off presumably to a bathroom. There was no separate kitchen. A basin, a kettle and a Calor Gas ring supplied her cooking needs. An empty and a half-full bottle of vodka stood beside them. The bed was a mattress on the floor with a sleeping bag on top, scrumpled as if its occupant had only just emerged. The whole place looked very studenty, in marked contrast to the impersonal tidiness of the flat over Polly's Cake Shop.

There were no pleasantries, no offers of drinks. Picking up from the conversation she'd had on the phone, Jude said, 'Your mother gave you an alibi for the whole of Saturday the third of October.'

'Oh, what did she say I was doing?'

'Spending the Sabbath with her at your grandmother's house.'

'Huh, the day you catch me doing that . . . Still, my mother is trying to help me for once, so perhaps I should be grateful for that.'

'If you weren't in Brighton that day,' asked Carole, 'then where were you?'

'I was actually here in the flat most of the day. Wish I'd stayed, given how things turned out, rather than going to Fethering.'

'And what made you go to Fethering?'

'A phone call. From Amos Green.'

'Had you spoken to him before?'

'No. I didn't recognize the name. But then he explained who he was.'

'What did he say?'

'He told me that he was trying to contact my mother, because they had been very close at one time. And he was in the Fethering area and he thought it'd be nice for them to meet up again "for old time's sake".'

'But he hadn't managed to contact her?'

'No. When she spends the Shabbat with Granny, she keeps her mobile phone switched off.'

'And then . . .?' Carole prompted.

'And then he started boasting about how close he'd been to my mother. He said they'd had an affair more than twenty years ago, but when she was already married to my father. And then they'd re-met in Fethering . . . eleven years later. And because my mother claimed she was in love with Amos, she told my father she wanted a divorce. Amos Green was the cause of my parents splitting up. But then he didn't stay around and he was the cause of my mother becoming so bitter and destructive. Amos Green was the cause of her breaking up any chance I had of keeping a relationship with my father.'

'Hudson Vale?' asked Jude.

'Of course Hudson Vale! So virtually everything that has been screwed up in my life has been caused by Amos Green.'

'So what did you do?' asked Carole quietly.

'I fixed to meet him at Polly's Cake Shop after closing time. And before I left here I got a gun.'

'How on earth did you do that? It's not easy just to pick up a gun.'

'It's easy if you've got the kind of friends I have in Brighton.' She spoke with a degree of pride; the pride of a middle-class girl who had reacted against the values of her upbringing. 'There are a couple of guys I used to hang around with who're very into the drug scene here.'

'Gang members?'

'You bet. No problem for one of them to lay their hands on a gun. He owed me a favour, anyway.'

'So,' asked Carole, 'you went to Fethering with the firm intention of killing Amos Green?'

'Yes,' the girl replied coolly. 'He had to pay for all the evil he had caused. But for him, my mother and father wouldn't have divorced. I'd still have a proper relationship with the father I love.'

Jude was tempted to say that that father loved her too, but didn't think it was quite the moment.

'So you duly met Amos Green at Polly's?'

'Yes. After everyone else had gone home.'

Carole and Jude exchanged looks. That had been a miscalculation on Rosalie's part, but again it wasn't the right moment to raise the matter.

'And when you met . . .?'

'I took him into the store room. I don't know why. Maybe I thought shooting him in there would make less mess.'

'And did you talk to him?'

'There wasn't much to say. I shot him through the temple. I was amazed how little blood there was.'

'Did you deliberately shoot him through the temple so that it could look like suicide?' asked Carole.

'I hadn't thought that far. All I knew was that I wanted him dead.'

'And what did you feel when you'd killed him?'

'I felt strange. Shocked perhaps, but also relieved. It was like a great weight had been lifted off my back.'

'So what did you do?'

'I put the gun on the window sill . . . not for any particular reason. I wasn't thinking of anyone finding it and wondering how it got there. I went out of the store room into the yard at the back, then through to the beach. I'd got the keys, of course. And then I just walked along the sands for a while. Feeling numb, really, but also euphoric. I don't know how long I was there.'

Long enough, thought Carole and Jude, for both Sara and Binnie to have time to look in the store room and see the body.

'Anyway, after a while I started thinking more practically. I had achieved what I'd wanted to achieve, I'd killed Amos Green. But now I needed to get rid of his body.

'Well, of course the sea was the obvious place. If I weighed his body down. But I couldn't just chuck him in from the shore. He'd get washed back on to the sand straight away. So I realized I'd need a boat to take him out to the deeper water. I could handle a boat. I used to be a member of the yacht club, until my mother decided I was meeting "the wrong kind of people" there.

'So I thought about who I knew with a boat that I could borrow.'

'And came up with the name of Kent Warboys?'

'Exactly. We'd had this affair for a time and I knew he felt guilty about the way he'd broken it off – particularly because he then got engaged so quickly to Sara Courtney. So I didn't have to put much pressure on him. He said I could borrow the rubber dinghy, so long as I put it back in his garden when I'd finished – and so long as I never told him what I needed it for.

'After it got dark, I picked up the rubber dinghy and rowed it along as near as I could get to Polly's back yard, moored it and then fetched the body. Bloody heavy, it was.

'I used some rope and bits of broken concrete I found in the yard and then dragged Amos Green to where the boat was. I rowed him out to beyond where I knew the seabed shelved and pushed him over the side.'

Rosalie Achter beamed in recognition of her achievement. 'And I felt my life had been cleansed,' she said.

'And didn't you feel any regret?' asked Jude.

'Good heavens, no.' There was a silence. 'Well, yes, there was one thing I regretted.'

'What?'

'I regretted I hadn't found some stronger rope to tie his body to the concrete. If I had, he'd still be down there.'

THIRTY-ONE

The police did become involved at that point. Rosalie Achter seemed unworried at the prospect of being charged with murder. She still thought what she had done was entirely logical and justifiable.

Jude persuaded Sara Courtney finally to tell her story to the police. She also handed over the handkerchief bearing the stain of Amos Green's blood. And testimony from Binnie confirmed what they had both seen in the store room of Polly's Cake Shop.

Rosalie Achter was duly arrested. She refused to let her mother come to see her in prison where she was awaiting trial, but she was very pleased that Hudson Vale, the man she still thought of as her father, visited her. That fractured relationship was one which was to heal over a long period of prison visiting. Later into her sentence, he also brought his second wife and twin daughters to meet her.

And when Rosalie came out of prison, having served the minimum term that the judge had given her, she spent a lot of time with her new family, the family she had always dreamed of while locked into the poisonous relationship she shared with her mother. And she appeared never to ask herself the question of who her birth father actually was.

Josie Achter she never saw again.

The fate of Polly's Cake Shop (as it was now renamed) was predictable. It did reopen (with no fanfare) under the management of Sara Courtney. The Volunteer Rota was very efficiently organized by Carole Seddon and, to her delight, Binnie returned to her waitressing duties. Carole surprised herself by how much she enjoyed being in charge of the volunteers. Maybe, for the first time in her life, she felt the tiniest tingling of Community Spirit.

And for a while the café worked well. But, from the financial point of view, it had always been a knife-edge operation and there was no surprise when, at the end of May, its final closure was announced.

The precipitating cause of this decision was a very happy one. Sara Courtney announced that she was pregnant. She and Kent were to be married in August. The marriage turned out to be a very successful one and, after ten years of looking after the children, Sara found the career she wanted running a restaurant in Fedborough that her husband had bought for her.

Less happy was the news in early June of Binnie Swale's death. In spite of all the memories in her house, without her work at Polly's, life had seemed empty to her. It turned out, from the dates on her funeral Order of Service, that she had been eighty-nine years old.

Things turned out better for Hammo the chef. After a couple of anxious months without work, he was taken on as assistant to Ed Pollack at the Crown and Anchor. And as the two young men shared recipes and experiments, the reputation of the pub's food grew even higher. People even booked from London to sample their menus.

Meanwhile Warboys Heritage Construction continued its development on the Polly's Cake Shop site. The upstairs flat was gutted and work began on the other two flats which would be built on the yard. Though at the planning stages, these dwellings had been proposed as 'affordable housing'; in the event they became rather higher spec than that. When the properties finally came on to the market, the estate agent's details described them as 'luxury accommodation'. So no young couples, 'brought up round here but unable to afford local prices' were able 'to stay in the area of their birth'. And of course Kent Warboys, having made a killing out of the café site, started eyeing up other retail and accommodation units along Fethering Parade with a view to further development.

As usual, he had done nothing illegal. His support for the SPCS Action Committee had been genuine; the twenty thousand he'd injected into the project had been real money. But he'd known from the start that all he had to do was sit and wait. The proposal for Polly's Community Café, ticking a lot of desirable boxes for the local authority, had speeded the passage of his larger designs through the planning process. But he knew it wouldn't last. Experience had told Kent that very few Community Projects of that kind survive more than a few months.

For a while the café part of the building remained closed. Then the announcement came that it would reopen in the New Year as a

Starbucks. This time no one in Fethering seemed to mind. Quintus Braithwaite felt no urgency to write again to the *Fethering Observer* about the threat of 'a genuinely local business becoming an identikit branch of an international, overpriced conglomerate with an idiosyncratic attitude to paying British taxes'. Nor did he and Phoebe form another protest group. The SPCS Action Committee was far away in their past. They had since moved their charitable focus from the welfare of abandoned donkeys in the Holy Land, via various other good causes, to the renovation as an arts centre of a pig sty that had once belonged to G. K. Chesterton.

(As to the expensive notepaper that Quintus had had designed for himself, having kept a few sheets back for his personal archive, he passed the rest on to Phoebe. She in her turn passed it on to one of her Joannas or Samanthas, who helped out with remedial reading at Fethering Primary School. So Quintus's fine letterhead ended up being scribbled on. If only the schoolchildren with their felt pens knew how much their scrap paper had cost per sheet.)

In fact some Fethering residents positively welcomed the news of Starbucks' forthcoming arrival, thinking it might make the village more upmarket and raise house prices. Who could say, one day Fethering might even get its own branch of Waitrose and its gentrification would be complete.

And for Carole and Jude, life went on in its usual way. The existence of her two gorgeous granddaughters animated Carole's life considerably.

And Jude continued the process of healing.